CHASING SHADOWS

BERNADETTE MARIE

 5 PRINCE PUBLISHING

CHASING SHADOWS

Bernadette Marie

5 PRINCE PUBLISHING & BOOKS, LLC

PO Box 16507

Denver, CO 80216

www.5PrinceBooks.com

ISBN-10:1-63112-197-9, ISBN-13:978-1-63112-197-5

CHASING SHADOWS. Bernadette Marie

Published by 5 Prince Publishing

Cover Credit: Viola Estrella

First Edition 2017

5 PRINCE PUBLISHING AND BOOKS, LLC.

For Stan,
No matter the crisis, you've always stuck by my side.
For that and a million other reasons, I love you.

ACKNOWLEDGMENTS

For my boys: Each day is a new adventure and you never know where it might take you. Remember the adventure. The good and bad ones, for they are the things that mold who you are.

For Mom, Dad, and Sissy: I love you. It's always good to know that when there is good or bad in my life, I can turn to you.

For Cate: This book has been our own brand of adventure, from new-to-me writing, to real-life drama unfolding around us. Your voice is important to me. Thank you for using it to make me shine.

For my fellow RMFW IPALers: The growth I have had since I became part of this group has been enormous. Thank you for your love, support, and words of wisdom when I'm looking for it.

For my Beta Readers: Thank you for volunteering to read me and help us in our quest to continue putting out good stories.

For my Readers: Without you, my stories would never grow. Thank you for following me on my journey and for being part of it.

Other titles by Bernadette Marie

THE KELLER FAMILY SERIES

The Executive's Decision

A Second Chance

Opposite Attraction

Center Stage

Lost and Found

Love Songs

Home Run

The Acceptance

The Merger

The Escape Clause

A Romance for Christmas

ASPEN CREEK SERIES

First Kiss

Unexpected Admirer

On Thin Ice

Indomitable Spirit

THE MATCHMAKER SERIES

Matchmakers

Encore

Finding Hope

THE THREE MRS. MONROES

Amelia

Penelope

Vivian

DENVER BRIDE SERIES

Candy Kisses

Cart Before the Horse

Never Saw it Coming

THE WALKER FAMILY SERIES

Walker Pride

Stargazing

Walker Bride

Wanderlust

Walker Revenge

Victory

Walker Spirit

STAND ALONE TITLES

Chasing Shadows

CHASING SHADOWS

Bernadette Marie

Icy fingers of cold air pressed against Declan Matthews' shirt as the wind blew through the trees. Once upon a time the wooded area, less than a mile from his childhood home, would have been a place of refuge. Now it was tainted with death.

The massive tree, which had been brought down by lightning at least fifty years earlier, still made for a perfect bridge over the cold brook that calmly passed beneath it.

It was there that they had found his sister. She had died on that bridge of nature, right where she'd once played as a child.

He heard the footsteps on the dry leaves behind him, but he didn't turn. There was no reason to.

Vaughn moved in beside him, just as an old friend would do, without a word.

They'd shared many hours together in this spot. It was more than a tree in the woods. It had been a pirate ship, a lunar landing site, and a jungle with man-eating monkeys. It had also been a place to camp and have long talks. Or when they'd gotten older, a place to sneak off with one of their dads' beers and a cigar. He'd brought Lacy Pratt out to the log once for a massive make out session, which ended successfully in his car later that night. Of course, that would only be the beginning of the women who refused to talk to him after a relationship ended.

Vaughn shoved his hands into the front pockets of his jeans and rocked back on his heels. "Christ, Declan. I don't even know what to say."

"There's nothing to say."

"I can't believe something like this would happen here. Everyone knows everyone. Who could have done this?"

Declan hated the small town mentality, even if the town was no longer small, as it had been in his early youth. Small was why he'd moved so far away. Ask anyone in a small town who could have done something like murder a married mother of two, and they'd tell you no one. Give them a name and they'd give you a million reasons that person was a saint. He appreciated living in a big city where everyone was guilty of something. He was a lawyer, so he knew what he was talking about. He'd put enough dead-beats away for a long time.

He clenched his fists to his side. "People talk, V. Someone will spill and I'll see them hang for it," he said through gritted teeth. And he meant it. He'd found great restraint in his job, but this wasn't part of his job. This was his little sister, and he'd take revenge if it meant finding the bastard that left her on that log, dead.

"Am I going to have to put a watch on you, Matthews?" The voice came from behind them and both men turned.

Of all people, Lacy Pratt moved toward them. A badge hung around her neck and a gun was holstered on her hip. She looked as if she'd walked out of a detective show on TV in her black slacks and starched white shirt. Her long locks, which he'd once tangled his fingers in, had been traded for a shorter cut that didn't quite hit her shoulders.

As she moved closer, she tucked her hair behind her ear.

"I'm really sorry about what happened. Stacy was a vital part of our community and a good friend," she said, her eyes locked on his.

He realized these were the first words she'd spoken to him in fifteen years. What a crappy thing to have to say.

"Thanks. What's all this?" He nodded toward her badge and she looked down.

"Detective Pratt. I'm working the case."

He felt those icy cold fingers on his back again, but this time the sharpness dug into his skin.

"How long have you been a detective?"

Lacy inched closer, her hands on her hips. "You got a problem with me and this case?"

"I have a problem with this case for sure." He mimicked her stance. "But I don't think that's what I asked. I asked you how long you've been a detective."

He saw the shift in her demeanor as her eyes softened. "Eight years."

"Are you good at your job?"

Her eyes narrowed. "Damn good."

"I'm glad to hear that. I want the S.O.B. caught and I want him to pay."

"We're doing everything we can to..."

"I want more. Someone killed my sister. That's not just something I'm going to forget very quickly. Not only that, they killed her five miles from her house and a mile from where she grew up. And why here? Why did they bring her here?"

Lacy turned to Vaughn. "Give us a minute, will ya?"

Vaughn exchanged looks with Declan, to which Declan gave him a nod to do as she'd asked. He was well aware of the others patrolling around the woods looking for anything that would tie someone to his sister's death. He sure as hell hoped they'd find something.

"Do you have any leads?" he asked looking toward the log

which he thought he might cut into fire wood and burn out of the sheer necessity of making it go away.

"Every single person around is a suspect at this point."

He shifted his glance to look at her standing next to him. He'd admit, for five-three, she was as intimidating as hell with her stance and gun.

"So you've begun questioning everyone?"

"We're doing our job, Matthews."

The last name thing wasn't sitting well with him. "Did you forget my first name?"

"I tried to forget everything about you, but here you are."

He let the stab at him sting as it was meant to. "Well, I'm here now. And I want to know what we're going to do."

"We're going to do our jobs and you're going to let us."

Declan ran his tongue over his teeth. "Get on it then. My family needs some closure."

Lacy pulled her phone from her pocket. "I have some questions for you. I'm going to record our conversation. You got a problem with it?"

"Ask away," he said, facing her and crossing his arms in front of him.

She pushed the button on her phone and then looked up at him. "Where were you yesterday at approximately four-thirty in the afternoon?"

Declan felt himself wince, and when he looked at her, he knew she'd caught that. What the hell did he have to lose?

"I was with my divorce lawyer."

The flash of amusement that lit in her eyes was hard to miss, but she kept her demeanor. "I'll need the name and location of the lawyer and the meeting."

"Fine."

"Divorced, huh? Sucks."

"Tell me about it. Since I've gone there, I've been divorced for two years now. But is seems my ex-wife thinks I withheld income stats from them and she'd like a little more of my hard-earned money. Let me also put out there that I actually walked in on her in my bed with her ex-husband whom she's planning on remarrying."

"Ouch. Kick to the balls, huh?"

"Exactly."

"Can't imagine you'd lie about that, but I still have to check it out."

"I'd expect you to be thorough." Declan dropped his arms and shoved his hands into his pockets. "I took the first flight out of New York this morning. There'll be a paper trail for you too."

"Good to know."

"I haven't been to see my parents yet. I came right here," he admitted. "Have you seen them?"

Her expression softened. "They're devastated."

"Of course."

"Your mom began to clean the house and your dad, well, I don't know how many shots he had."

"What about Tom?"

Lacy tucked her phone back into her pocket. "Yeah, we talked to him. I've been at this a long time, and I've never seen a man as big as him break down as he did. One of those things that'll stick with me."

"Genuine shock?"

She nodded. "Yeah. I suggested maybe he should even go to the hospital. But he refused."

"The kids?"

"They were sleeping by the time we got to him. The department sent counselors over this morning to be there."

Declan pinched the bridge of his nose as a headache began to creep in. "They don't deserve this. No one deserves to live without their mother."

Lacy reached out and touched his arm. "I know how it feels. They'll be okay, but they'll never forget."

Declan lifted his gaze. "I forgot you grew up without your mother. I'm sorry."

"It's why I do what I do. There's a lot of sick people out there, Matthews. I'm here to stop them, and someday no kid will lose their mother like this."

"Maybe you should have gone to talk to my niece and nephew."

She tucked a fallen strand of hair behind her other ear. "If they need me I'll be there. They're good kids."

He nodded in agreement. "I should head to my parents' house. What happens now?"

She expelled a long breath. "We will need someone to positively identify her."

Declan squeezed his eyes closed then opened them slowly. "You really need that?"

"I'm afraid so. Tom said he'd do it, but..."

"I'll do it," he offered. "Dear God, never thought it would be something I'd do, but I'll do it."

Lacy pulled her card from her pocket and handed it to him. "Go to your folks and get settled in. I can meet you in town when you're ready."

He looked down at the Rolex on his wrist, which once was a big deal and now meant crap to him in the scheme of things. "I'll meet you there at three?"

"I'll be there," she confirmed. "Give my condolences to your family."

"I will."

She hesitated for a moment, then shot him a sympathetic smile before she left him alone again with the cold blowing through the trees.

2

I nside the confines of the car, Lacy closed her eyes and rested her head against the back of her seat. There was a hard exterior to her, and no one would ever see anything different. But when she was alone, she could let it crumble.

She'd just asked Stacy's brother to identify her dead body. That part of her job hurt each time she had to do it.

Lacy had identified her. She'd looked right into her lifeless eyes, but they needed a relative to verify and Tom was in no shape to do so. Declan seemed like the right choice.

There was a crushing pain in her chest and she rubbed the heel of her hand between her breasts to make it go away. Her memories of her own father coming home after identifying her mother would always flood back into her mind at these times. That was an image she would never get out of her mind. It had absolutely wrecked the man. Though he'd been an attentive and doting father, he'd always been broken.

The man had never dated another woman. The woman he'd loved with all his heart had been murdered. Nothing could replace his wife. Of course, Lacy hadn't done much to ease his pain when she decided to become a police officer, but it was something she had to do. If she could stop the senseless crimes on the street, she'd have done the world a service. But that daydream hadn't lasted long. Now she spent her days over the dead bodies of victims. Only sometimes she knew them.

Lacy raked her fingers into her hair and massaged her head.

Stacy had been a friend since high school. She was two years Lacy's junior, but they'd played volleyball together for years. When Stacy's kids had gotten old enough to be in school, she'd taken a job as a barista at the Starbucks only a block from Lacy's office. They'd become casual friends, shared a few dinners, and went out for girls' night out. She'd met Stacy's husband Tom many times, and when her son Toby needed to interview someone for a first grade class project, he'd chosen Lacy—and that had only been last month. Perhaps they'd become more than casual friends. And today she'd photographed her dead body draped over the log near the creek where Lacy had once made out with Stacy's brother—Declan.

There were days she absolutely hated her job. This was certainly one of those times. It usually brought the thought of her mother's death to mind. Much like Stacy, Lacy's mother had been found in a wooded area. If there was an upside to all of this, at least Stacy had only been there for a few hours. Her mother had been missing for weeks before a bunch of kids found her body when they'd gone to a hidden rope swing.

She felt her throat tighten with tears. There were two more children who would now grow up without their mother.

Lacy sat up in her seat and gripped her steering wheel. With a twist of her hands she heard the vinyl beneath her hands. As God was her witness, she would find the person responsible for this. Every person she came in contact with would be a suspect. And even though Declan Matthews seemed to have a solid alibi, she'd still keep a close eye on him. It wouldn't be the first case she'd had where a jealous sibling did something so horrific.

Turning the key in the ignition, Lacy started the car and

pulled away from the scene. It was time for her to pay her respects to Stacy's parents, and do a little digging there as well.

❧

DECLAN FIGURED HIMSELF FOR A STRONG MAN—AT LEAST UNTIL that morning. When the call had come in that his sister had been found dead—murdered—he'd actually thrown up. What strong man does that?

And standing in the place where they'd found her body, that hadn't helped his toughness any. That area had been a place of refuge as a child. Now it would forever be haunted by the thought that someone ended his sister's life there—or at least left her there.

He hadn't been ready to head to his parents' house quite yet. They weren't expecting him until the evening, so he was going to take some time to gain control over his emotions before trying to bring them some calm.

He'd ended up at the Starbucks where his sister had worked. In fact, he could hear the whispers of the employees as they each found out something had happened to Stacy. No one knew him, so he was but a fly on the wall. There was some solace in the fact that they were all deeply upset.

Declan watched the clientele that came and went. A few people asked about Stacy by name and the unfortunate employee who had been approached lost it.

He swirled his drink in his cup, not really thirsty for what he'd ordered.

As the door opened to the store, he watched Lacy walk in. Declan eased his arms onto the table and leaned in to focus on her.

There wrona a no-nonsense demeanor about her and he wondered how he'd ever gotten her in the back of his car. If he remembered correctly, he hadn't had to try too hard. But that was a long time ago. She was a broken spirit back then, but she seemed to have control over that now. Just the sight of her scared the hell out of him.

He assumed she was completely muscle under that black jacket. Her badge still hung around her neck and her handcuffs and gun were still holstered to her side. Why in the hell did that make his skin flush with heat?

She ordered her drink, shifted her eyes to each employee in the store, and then turned at the counter to check out the patrons.

It hadn't taken long before she caught his eye and her lips pursed.

She collected her drink and headed toward him. "I just came from your parents' house. You haven't been there yet," she said lifting her cup toward her mouth.

"Couldn't make myself go," he admitted. "I needed a few more minutes."

Lacy watched him over the top of her cup, then set it down on the table, and took the seat across from him. "I want you to take your mom to the doctor. She's extremely shaken up. She's faking it well, and your dad is enabling her, but..."

"I get it."

"Is there anything I can do for you?" she offered and Declan was sure his mouth had fallen open. "This is devastating for a family. I know that the kindness of others was all that got me and my dad through this same thing."

Declan rubbed his eyes and rested his head in his hand for a moment before lifting to look at her. "How long before the pain goes away?"

"You'll have that forever. I wish I could tell you it'll get easier. But it won't. You'll just learn to cope."

"I want to be strong enough when I see her kids. How does a kid deal with that?"

She reached her hand across the table and covered his. "We

learn. We lash out. We blame the world for our problems. We survive. And then we make the most out of it," she said, making sure he knew she was the expert here.

"It sounds like they'll have a long road in front of them."

"They will," she said retracting her hand. "But they have your family and Tom's family. They have this community, too." Lacy sipped her coffee. "Are you sticking around for a bit, or are you headed right back to New York?"

"I don't know how I'll concentrate on anything if I head back," he said running his hand over the back of his neck. "I suppose I'll stick around for a bit."

She gave him a curt nod and stood. Picking up her coffee, she locked eyes with him. "I'm curious as to why someone would have chosen that spot to leave her," she said.

"I wonder that too. Very few of us knew about it."

"I'd like to talk to you about it later. When you come down to the station at three, maybe we could chat."

"Sure. I want to be of any help I can be."

"Go see your folks," she said, as she turned and left the store.

Declan wrapped his hands around his cup and stared down into it. It was inevitable. He had to go to them.

When he looked up, a young man perhaps twenty, stood where Lacy had looking down at him. His green Starbucks apron had obviously seen its share of spills during the day.

"I was told you're Stacy's brother," the man's voice shook as he spoke.

"You heard right."

"Is she really dead?"

Declan supposed he'd have to get used to peoples' reaction to the news of his sister. Certainly this wouldn't be the only person who would approach him.

"That's what they tell me," he said, realizing his answer was cold and perhaps a bit heartless. "I'm going to see her in a bit," he added, as if that could take the chill out of his words.

"I'm sick over it. Just sick," the man said and lifted a shaky hand to his glasses to push them up on his nose. "I thought that last girl was only a fluke."

"Last girl?"

"Yeah, they found another girl about two months ago in the same area."

"Who told you where they found her?"

The man wiped his hands on his apron. "Police were talking to some of the people who worked with Stacy yesterday."

"What's your name?" Declan asked.

"Carter, sir."

"Thanks for the information, Carter. I'll make sure my family leaves word with the store when they have her memorial. I'm sure she had a lot of friends here."

Carter nodded. "Everyone loved her."

And if anything could warm Declan's heart right now, it was that. "Thanks."

Carter gave him a nervous smile, and went back to work.

3

The moment the front door opened, his mother fell into his arms and sobbed. He held her tightly, as if to hold her up because she no longer could stand on her own.

It broke his heart. He'd never seen his mother this weak.

He eased her into the house and noticed his father seated in his chair staring blankly in front of him.

"Hi, Dad," he said as he held on tightly to his mother.

"You didn't come here first," he snarled without blinking or looking in Declan's direction.

"No. I'm sorry about that. I wanted to go to the scene. I needed to wrap my head around it." He walked his mother to her chair and eased her down before kneeling before her to speak to her. "Detective Pratt wants me to take you to the hospital."

His mother's eyes shifted to him and then to the floor before his father spoke. "She's fine. We're just in shock."

"Yeah, well I think Detective Pratt is right." He looked up at his mother again. "I'm going to get your things and take you. Dad, why don't you go with us."

For the first time since he'd walked in the door, his father looked at him, but he'd have sworn he looked right though him. "I don't need to go."

"I meant come to support mom." He stood without an answer from him. "I'll get her stuff. I assume your coat and your purse are in the same place as always?"

His mother nodded and he started toward the mudroom on the back of the kitchen.

Things were certainly out of order, he noticed as he walked through the house. It looked as though breakfast had been burnt, and not cleaned up, even though Lacy said she'd begun cleaning immediately. There were more coffee mugs in the sink than the usual two.

Declan went to the closet by the back door and opened it. His mother's purse sat on a shelf and her coat hung right next to it, just as it always had. That gave him some comfort. One thing in his life hadn't changed, and he'd take it, no matter how insignificant it was.

An hour and a half later, they had checked his mother into a room for observation. But Declan knew that they were equally as attentive to his father who sat in the chair in the corner.

The nurse who attended to his mother had given her something to calm her, brought her some tea, and a warm blanket. And somehow, she'd managed to get his father to talk and accept a cup of coffee, which she assured Declan was decaf.

When his parents were settled she walked Declan to the hallway.

"They'll be okay. We often see this when people of their age have received devastating news. As soon as they can be calm for a bit, their bodies will adjust. We want to keep your mother until tomorrow morning, and I'll make your father equally as comfortable."

"I appreciate this. I really do." He looked at his watch. "I'm supposed to meet the detective."

"Go. I'll call you if anything comes about."

He gave the nurse a nod and headed out to his car.

Once he was behind the wheel, he sat for a moment. How had everything come to this, he wondered? His parents had never done anything to deserve this—and neither had his sister.

He took a self-inventory to see what he was feeling. Deep down his body ached and it was caused by an anger he couldn't yet release. He could only assume that once he looked at his sister, it might surface. God forbid he should run into her murderer. If he did, they'd surely have two bodies on their hands, because nothing would stop him from taking the life of the person who took his sister's.

Declan drove downtown to Detective Lacy Pratt's office. The sheer size of the department told him that a lot had changed since he'd grown up there. Once upon a time, the police department was a small building with three cars. Now it was a multi-level building with a gated area where they kept a fleet of cars.

Well, he thought, if they needed that much protection for their citizens then perhaps it was possible they had a murderer in their midst. He could only hope Lacy was good at her job and would catch the S.O.B. And at that moment, he vowed to stay in town until they did.

LACY TAPPED HER FINGER AGAINST THE WHITE FOAM CUP OF coffee as she looked over the report she'd typed up. Paperwork was a bitch. She should be out there, trying to find out what happened to Stacy, but first things first—paperwork.

Her hands were shaking from the amount of coffee she'd consumed already today. It was very possible she'd forgotten to eat.

As she stared at her computer screen, the motion of someone walking up to her desk caught her eye. She looked up to find Declan standing there, and he looked broken.

She'd kept tabs on him over the years, though she wouldn't tell him that. The last time they'd spoken, she had made it very clear that she'd never wanted to see him, or talk to him again. Up until today, that vow had stayed intact.

The dark eyes she'd once found so dreamy were now hollow. His shoulders hunched, and she'd heard the shuffle of his walk.

"Didn't think cops had desks," he said as he sat down in the chair on the other side of her desk.

"Detective," she reminded him. "It makes it more comfortable to write up reports and talk to witnesses."

He looked around the room that was scattered with desks and men and women working. "Witnesses have to talk to you in the open like this?"

"If it's something better discussed in private we use a conference room."

He nodded and she wondered why he was so surprised by her surroundings when, as a lawyer, he had to have seen his share of police stations.

Lacy stood and pushed back her chair. "I suppose we should get this over with," she said and his gaze followed her. "Are you okay to do this?"

His eyes managed to grow even darker and sadder. "No. No, I'm not okay," he replied as he stood, balancing himself with his hands still on her desk. "But I'm going to. It's the least I can do for her. Just tell me," he paused and took a breath. "Is she bad?"

Instinct had her reaching out to cover his hand with hers. "She looks perfect, and that's what gets me," she admitted as she withdrew her hand. "There's some slight bruising, but otherwise she looks as though she might have fallen in the woods and died."

"Could that have been what happened?"

Lacy walked around her desk to his side. "No."

"Too bad. That would have made a better story," he sighed, as he followed her to the elevator. He turned toward her as the door closed. "How did she die?"

Lacy swallowed hard. She'd have expected him to ask when

they'd called him. Perhaps there was a reason he hadn't, or maybe the lawyer in him was double checking the facts that he had.

She pushed her shoulders back and looked up at the numbers counting down on the elevator as they descended.

"Awaiting autopsy, of course," she shifted to look at him and he nodded in understanding. "It looks as though she was strangled."

As strange as it seemed, she could see the slightest bit of tension slip from him. His shoulders dropped and he nodded slowly. Perhaps he'd been expecting a gruesome detail he wasn't ready to handle.

She'd seen her share of those kinds of murders and it was never her favorite part of the job to tell someone that their loved one had been stabbed, shot, or dismembered.

As the elevator slowed, she thought of the few times when her job was an actual joy. Those moments were sparse, and yet she showed up to work every day with hope that she'd help save someone or put a dangerous criminal behind bars. Often, though, she escorted an innocent family member to the basement to identify their loved one. And when they crumbled she drew from her mother's compassion, which she remembered from her childhood, and she would embrace the loved one that was left behind. And each time, she would vow to bring them comfort by finding the guilty party.

There were times when she took her holster and badge off each day that she wondered if she was a detective to help others, or if she was still searching for that comfort for herself.

When the doors opened, Lacy stepped out of the elevator first. She looked at the dimly lit, gray hallway and considered that if it were a bit brighter and perhaps painted with a cheery yellow, it wouldn't mimic the mood of the person making the walk toward the room of steel, cold drawers where their loved ones awaited.

They came to the room where Stacy's body would be laid out for them. She'd called the M.E. before Declan had arrived.

She reached for the door knob, but then pulled away her hand. Turning toward Declan, she inhaled deeply.

"Listen, I know this isn't easy to do. I hate asking people to do it, especially since I knew the deceased, but..."

"I get it. I've escorted a few clients through this myself. I'll be okay."

Respect for Stacy had Lacy reaching for Declan's hand and giving it a squeeze. "I'm going to find the bastard. I swear it."

He looked down at her hand covering his. "I know you will. I have no doubt you're fantastic at your job. I've been on the wrong side of your temper, remember."

Lacy winced. "When we're done here, can I buy you a drink? I think if I'm going to work this case, maybe we'd better clear the air."

"I need to go to Tom and the kids."

"Right. Of course you do."

His hand turned under hers and he held it in his. "Dinner? Eight o'clock. Harvey's."

"I'll be there," she agreed. Pulling her hand from his, she turned and opened the door.

DECLAN THOUGHT IT WOULDN'T BOTHER HIM TO WALK INTO the room and see his sister, but when Lacy pushed open the door he froze in the hallway.

She turned back to him. "I can show you a photo instead."

Shaking his head, he took his first step and a moment later was standing in the room with his sister only a few feet away.

Her face was exposed, though her body was concealed. Her blonde hair looked dirty, though her face had been cleaned.

Declan inched closer. "Doesn't even look like her, does it?"

"All I need to know is if it's positively her."

"Butterfly tattoo on the inside of her right wrist."

Lacy nodded. "That's confirmed."

"I know that it's her. I just don't want to say that it is." For the first time since he'd received the call, he felt the stinging of tears behind his eyes, and he could see no reason to fight them.

Declan tried to blink them away, but they fell from his eyes and streaked over his cheeks before he could wipe them away.

This was his baby sister he was looking at laying there before him. Her lifeless body offered absolutely no hope that it was a huge mistake.

"When will we have the information from the autopsy?"

"There are some initial findings. The toxicology reports will take longer."

He raised his head and turned it slightly so that Lacy wouldn't see his tear-filled eyes. "Why did they do toxicology reports?"

"We need to know if she was drugged, drunk, on drugs."

"My sister would never do drugs."

"I don't believe she would either."

Declan raised his hand with all intent to touch his sister's cheek, but he retracted it, unable to bring himself to touch her. "What happens now?"

"We'll release the body to her husband and then your family can go about making funeral arrangements."

"It doesn't seem right to do that if her killer isn't caught."

He caught the sniffle from her, and he realized she too was having a hard time dealing with what was happening, even though she saw this every day.

"We won't quit working on this just because she's buried. Your family needs closure. Her children need it. Once the funeral home has her body, they can make her look as though she's sleeping. It'll help the kids to say goodbye to her if she looks like that."

He realized that by taking on the identifying of her body, he'd be the only one in the family to have nightmares of her in this state.

Finally, he reached his hand to her and touched her frozen skin. "We'll find who did this, Stacy. No other person will suffer. No other family," he promised her and then felt Lacy's hand touch his shoulder.

"They have her personal effects. You can sign for them. Her car is being processed. But when it's done, the family can have it as well."

"Where was her car?"

"Still in the parking lot on the west side of the trail. That empty lot where kids would park," she cleared her throat, "they made it into a parking lot for the open space. It appears she was running on the trail."

He nodded and stepped away from his sister. Inside, his stomach churned and an anger he'd never felt began to brew in his veins. God help the person who did this to his sister. If he ever came face to face with them, he'd kill the son of a bitch.

❧ 4 ❧

A small paper bag sat on the seat of Declan's rented car. Everything they had that was with his sister when they found her was contained in that bag, except for her clothes and phone which they'd kept in evidence.

Her wedding ring, he'd carry that into her house with him and hand it to her husband. There was a headband, a small pair of earrings, her fitness monitor watch thing, and her driver's license which had been tucked behind her phone.

When he pulled up in front of his sister's house, he parked across the street.

Declan felt his pocket to make sure the ring was inside as he stepped out of the car. As he shut the door, the shine from his shoes caught his attention. He was still wearing the suit he'd been wearing when they'd called him. At some point, he was going to have to go buy new clothes. And he was probably going to have to burn this suit, because he wouldn't want to remember this day every time he wore it.

Crossing the street, he noticed his nephew on the front step. He hadn't seen him when he'd driven up.

"Hey, big guy," Declan said so that Toby could hear him.

When the young boy lifted his sad eyes to look at his uncle, it tore Declan into a million pieces.

He didn't say anything, but he stood, and walked directly to Declan, who scooped him up and held him tightly.

Declan was great in court. He could say all the right things to the right people and make problems go away. But what was he supposed to say to a seven-year-old who rested his head on his shoulder for comfort?

He opted for not saying anything, and just let Toby cling to him for as long as necessary.

As Declan carried him toward the steps, the front screen opened and Tom stood looking down at them.

"Declan, thanks for coming," Tom said holding the door open as an invitation to enter. "This has been... well a shitty day is the only way to put it."

"Couldn't agree more," he offered as he carried Toby into the house. "How are you holding up?"

Tom shrugged. "I'm numb. I keep waiting to wake up and have her standing there with a cup of coffee telling me I'm late." He smiled as it must have been a fond memory that had made him say that. "You saw her?"

And now it was Declan's moment to ruin that fine thought that they'd all wake up and this nightmare wouldn't be real. "I did."

He felt Toby cling to him tighter and he realized this certainly wasn't the time for this conversation. When he looked back at Tom, he saw the tears welling in the man's eyes. He was glad that the next time they all saw Stacy she'd have been made to look like she was sleeping. As it was, his memory of her would always be skewed.

"My folks are in the kitchen with Andi. She's five-years-old, Dec. She doesn't really understand all of this. I've been working on getting in touch with the insurance and the funeral home. So much to think about."

"I'm here for the duration, Tom. Whatever I can do to assist you, I'm here."

As if the man had run out of words, Tom simply nodded and walked toward the kitchen.

Declan wondered if Toby had fallen asleep on his shoulder, as his tiny body had suddenly become so much heavier. But he followed Tom.

Tom's mother, Janice, rose from where she sat with Andi and moved to him. Disregarding the boy in his arms, she wrapped her arms around both of them. "Oh, Declan. I'm so sorry about your sister. This is horrible."

"I'm still in a bit of shock," he admitted, realizing that for the first time, someone wanted to console him. "Thanks for driving down to be with them."

"They're going to need us for a bit. We'll be here."

Declan was pleased to hear that. His own parents weren't going to be of much help. They could hardly keep themselves together. And that reminded him, he needed to stop by the hospital and check back in with his mother. Maybe he should cancel dinner with Lacy. Then again, he could sure use some company that wasn't family. He'd keep the dinner plans.

Janice rested her hand on Toby's back. "I think all of this has exhausted him. Poor boy fell asleep."

Declan had his confirmation. "I'll go put him on his bed."

"You know which one it is?"

He nodded and started up the stairs with the boy who was growing heavier by the moment.

Yes, he knew which room. When Toby was born, Declan had made sure to visit once a month, when he could. He didn't want to miss out on his nephew's first year. He was sure he'd never have kids of his own, so he needed to create a bond with his sister's kids.

Stacy's presence hit him hard when he walked into Toby's room. She'd decorated it all herself when she was seven months pregnant with him. It was a Cars theme, and she must have known he'd grow to adore that movie. Lightning McQueen comforters and pillows adorned the bed. Mater toys and posters decorated the room. He had to smile when he saw a Woody doll in the corner. Childhood was too short to only embrace one classic.

He laid Toby on the bed, and pulled the comforter up around him. For a moment he stood and stared at him. He had Stacy's blonde hair and Tom's curls. Declan couldn't imagine how much he'd love his own children, if he were to have them. These children were his world.

As he left Toby's room, he pulled the door closed slightly and headed back downstairs.

Janice was busy at the stove now, making the family dinner. Andi was coloring in a princess coloring book, which Declan recognized as one he'd sent her for Valentine's Day. Maurice, Tom's father, was seated at the table with Andi, with a notebook by his side and his laptop in front of him.

"Where's Tom?"

Janice looked up from the pot she'd filled with water and set on the stove. "I think he's in his office. He's having a hard time keeping his emotions under control around the kids."

"I can't even imagine."

Declan walked to the small home office near the front of the house and tapped on the open French door.

"Hey, Declan. Come in. I'm just going through these messages that are cluttering up my phone. I should call everyone back but..."

"They can wait. You can take all the time in the world to respond, if you ever feel like doing so."

"Yeah. I suppose." Tom put his hands in his curly hair and stopped as he stared down at a small stack of papers laying on the desk. "This is all so overwhelming. I don't even know where to start with everything."

Declan moved into the room and stood next to the desk. "I'd be more than happy to help you sort through everything and make arrangements."

"You would?"

"Of course."

Tom dropped his hands. "This sucks for you and I think we keep forgetting that. She was your sister. An intricate part of your entire life. You shouldn't have to be in constant control."

"My job offers me an expertise in constant control even if it's something that isn't pleasant."

Tom turned to him, tucked his hands into the pockets of his jeans, and looked up at Declan with red, swollen eyes. "How did she look?" Then he shook his head. "No. I don't want to know."

Declan reached out and rested his hand on Tom's shoulder. "She looked as though she was resting," he offered, and felt as though it wasn't a complete lie.

"He killed her," Tom growled through his teeth. "That son-of-a-bitch killed her."

Declan gripped Tom's shoulder tighter. "Who?"

"I don't know," he cried, and the tears poured down his cheeks. "Murdered. Not just some accident, but someone took my wife's life. Murder."

"We'll know more soon, Tom. Lacy Pratt is working the case and..."

"God, that's awfully personal."

Declan dropped his hand. "Why's that?"

Tom wiped his eyes. "They were friends. Girls' nights out. Coffee dates. Toby even interviewed her for a class project a few weeks ago."

"I didn't realize they were such good friends."

"You've been gone a long time, Declan."

And that was the truth. "Speaking of Lacy, I'm meeting her tonight to talk. I can come back here after if you need someone to talk to."

Tom let out a long hard breath. "I'm so exhausted. Honestly, I just want to have a shot of whiskey and pass out."

Declan couldn't help but chuckle. "One shot will do that?"

"At this point, God, I hope so."

"I'm glad your folks are here."

"So am I. They've kept us together." He looked up and this time his eyes had gone wide. "Oh, God, how are your parents? I haven't talked to them. I didn't go to them. I'm horrible. I should have gone to them."

Declan held up his hands. "You're all going to process this on your own. Tomorrow will come soon enough when we all have to sit down and mourn together."

"I feel terrible."

"I took Mom to the hospital earlier today. They were keeping her to observe her."

Tom shook his head. "I can't imagine losing your child."

And that had been a different thought that nearly paralyzed Declan altogether.

"Call me if you need me," he said reaching his hand into his pocket and pulling out Stacy's wedding ring. "I need to give this to you."

"This is Stacy's."

"I signed for her belongings. The police still have her phone, her clothes, and her car."

"Whoever did this didn't steal her ring?" he asked, looking at the nearly two carat ring that he held up to the light.

"No. Did the police tell you it had been stolen?"

Tom shook his head. "No, it's just, if someone is going to kill someone, don't they take their valuables? On some freaking path while she was running, her phone and this ring were all the valuables she had. Why not take the fricking ring?"

He almost sounded angry that they hadn't robbed her. Then again, maybe it would have made sense then—if murder could make sense.

"I don't know. Keep it safe. Someday maybe Andi would like to have it."

His words sparked more tears from Tom, and he pulled him in for a hug. "I'll be back in the morning. Get some rest."

Tom nodded. "Thanks for everything. Especially your cool head."

Declan chuckled. "It's all I have."

⚜

LACY SAT AT THE TABLE AT HARVEY'S LOOKING AT HER WATCH. Hadn't they said eight o'clock? He was already nearly twenty minutes late.

She'd ordered a beer, drank it, and now was contemplating another when she saw him walk in.

The day must have taken its toll on him, she thought as he walked toward her. His once crisp dress shirt was wrinkled. His hair looked as though his fingers had tunneled through it a million times. Dark circles made his eyes look sunken, and the shadow of a beard had darkened his face.

"Sorry I'm late. I was at my sister's house," he said offering his apology as he sat down across from her.

"How are they?"

"A wreck," he admitted as he signaled for the waitress and ordered himself a beer and Lacy ordered another. "Tom's parents are there, helping keep some normality and calm."

"That's very nice. How's your mom doing?"

"I'll head to the hospital after this to check on her."

"When will you sleep?"

"When this is all over."

The waitress brought their beers and took their dinner order. Lacy ordered an appetizer of wings and Declan, out of habit, ordered a cheeseburger with ketchup only.

"Listen, Matthews, I know that we haven't spoken in forever. I think now that I'm going to be embedded in your life for a while, I should apologize to you and reiterate that I'm good at my job and I have your family's best interests in mind."

"Did I make it seem as if you weren't going to be able to handle this?"

"Most of the people I deal with, I haven't had sex with."

That statement obviously caught him off guard. He reached for his beer and took a long pull. His eyes were wide, and she knew she'd thrown him for a loop with her apology.

"That was a very long time ago. We were young and didn't know what we were doing. And I can't believe you're apologizing. C'mon, I was a teenage boy who managed to get you in the back of my car. I should be apologizing for that."

She shook her head. "Well, you don't have to. But, let's just say, I was in that car due to my background. Due to my mother's death. Due to what it did to me as child." She reached across the table and took his hand. "Promise me one thing. Promise me you'll convince Tom to get the kids some counseling."

He looked at her hand on his, then back up at her. "I'll make sure to talk to him about it," he agreed and she pulled back her hand, smiling, satisfied with that.

She wasn't ready to go into detail with him, but for years she felt as though she'd used him. She'd used a lot of people back then to get what she wanted—what she needed. Now, in her line of work, she felt as though, somehow, she was giving back. Even if it was just the littlest bit. If someone would gain comfort from her loss, then everything had a reason—even sex in the back of Matthews' car.

The waitress returned with their meals and set them on the table. Declan ordered another beer, and she a cup of coffee.

Situating her plate in front of her, and turning it so it faced just right, she picked up a wing and dredged it through the ranch dressing. "Where are you staying?" she asked, as he pulled the unwanted pickles off his hamburger.

"You know, I have no idea. I left my office with nothing but my wallet. I didn't make plans with my parents or with Tom. I didn't do anything but rent a car when I got here. I still have to buy some clothes, after I go to the hospital."

"You're going to pass out from exhaustion, Matthews."

"It might be the only way I get some sleep."

"Understood." She wiped her mouth and decided that buffalo wings were not the item to order when a good-looking man was going to be dining with you. Of course, she hadn't been thinking about being impressive either.

Declan pinched the bridge of his nose and then rubbed his eyes. "Shit, I hope I gave my assistant enough information when I ran out. I haven't even checked my phone in hours to see if anyone called me."

"I'm sure they'd understand. This is an extreme situation, Matthews."

"Maybe I'll call Vaughn and see if I can crash at his place. Maybe he'll lend me some clothes, too," he said as if his mind were skipping around.

She understood that. Her mind had been doing that as well since she'd received the call and saw Stacy laying on that log—that same log which had once held memories for her, too.

After having taken three bites out of his hamburger, he pushed his plate away.

"Not hungry?" she asked as she scooped another wing through the ranch.

"That's the first thing I've eaten since I had a bagel at six o'clock this morning. And that was east coast time." He raked his fingers through his already tunneled hair. "It was a normal morning. I got up, went to the gym, grabbed a cup of coffee and a bagel on my way back to my condo. Showered, shaved," he added as he ran his hand over his chin. "Took a cab to work since I wanted to get there earlier than if I took the subway. I walked in, gave Abul a high five, and went straight to my office for a half hour to go over the documents I'd left unfinished. Went to my morning meeting, and that was when I got the call. I left everything on the table in the conference room and walked right out of the building."

"Do you want some coffee? I could order you some coffee," she offered as she watched him begin to break down. It was normal, she reminded herself. The strong ones usually had to cave at some point.

"I'm fine," he said as he pulled his phone from his pocket. "No wonder I haven't had any other calls. It's dead."

"Who are you calling?"

"Vaughn."

"I have his number." She pulled her phone from her back pocket and handed it to him. "He's in my contacts."

"Thanks," he said as he scrolled through her phone. Then he shifted his eyes to her. "Why do you have his number in your phone?"

"We live in the same town, Matthews."

"But you're friends?"

She wiped her mouth again, and set the napkin in her lap. "No. As a matter of fact, we're not friends. I happen to find him appalling, annoying, and rude."

He actually laughed at that. "That's Vaughn. Still, why do you have his number?"

"He witnessed a hit and run once. I questioned him. Stood to reason to keep the number."

Declan nodded and pushed the phone number. Lacy waited for him to finish his phone call. She couldn't help but wonder if Vaughn thought his friend was high from the way his conversation hopped from one subject to another. She knew it was absolute exhaustion.

"Looks like I have a couch for the night."

She took her phone back when he offered it and tucked it back in her pocket. "Good. You should head over there now. Get some sleep. It looks like her car will be released tomorrow. They found nothing in it."

"Okay. You'll call me?"

"I will," she promised.

He reached into his pocket and pulled out his wallet.

"Matthews, put your money away. I've got this."

"Nah, I can't let you do that."

"You've got enough on your mind. I can buy you a beer and a burger, which I'm taking home with me since you didn't eat it at all."

He chuckled and slid out of the booth. "Thanks. I appreciate everything."

"Don't thank me until I have cuffs on the asshole that brought you back here."

"I'll thank you then, too."

"Get some sleep. Some good sleep."

He nodded and gave her a small wave as he left the restaurant and headed to the parking lot.

Lacy watched him until he pulled away, then she slouched in the booth, and rested her head against it. She hoped Declan didn't spiral down the same path her father did. When her mother died, nothing seemed important to him anymore—except for her. But Lacy was a handful, and she gave him plenty to worry over.

She waved down the waitress, asked for the check, and a carryout container.

As she boxed up the hamburger, she thought about Declan's reaction when she'd apologized for not talking to him for the past fifteen years. Had it mattered to him that she'd gone cold and callous after their childish affair? Had he even noticed?

What did it matter now? The truth was she had a job to do. There was a murderer on the loose in her town and he'd killed a dear friend. They weren't quite twelve hours into the investigation, and they still had no leads. He'd been careful—too careful.

That meant he was an expert when it came to killing people and leaving no tracks, or he was a novice who had planned this out meticulously. But what she didn't understand was why Stacy? What could anyone gain from killing her?

Lacy wiped her hands over her eyes, then drank down her coffee. It was nearly nine-thirty, but she was headed back to head-quarters. There was no sleep for her either. She needed to go over the evidence and reports one more time for her own sanity. It was, however, gnawing at her—what had Vaughn been doing there this morning? He'd been questioned in another murder in the same area, and his presence there this morning wasn't sitting well with her.

5

Vaughn stood at the door and waited for Declan to cross the street. It was nearly eleven-thirty, and Declan thought he was going to pass out in the middle of the yard. He'd never in his life been so tired, and he'd done a lot of all-nighters in college, but still—never.

"Buddy, you look like hell," Vaughn's greeting was less than cheery. "What did Pratt do to you?"

Declan chuckled. "You know what she did? She apologized for being a bitch after our little *thing* in high school."

Vaughn stepped back so that Declan could walk through the door, then he shut and locked it. "She apologized to you? You were a teenage boy. The only thing on your mind was getting a girl to have sex with you."

"Yeah," he said shaking his head. "I guess after fifteen years she was the one who hurt me in the deal."

Vaughn shook his head. "Doesn't even make sense, dude. It's not like you didn't try dating. You were interested. I remember."

He smiled. "I was interested. There was something about her —still is."

Now Vaughn smiled back. "Seriously? You got a thing for the cop?"

Declan rubbed the tension from his neck. "No. She's just tough, and I like a gal who can stand up for herself."

"Yeah, well I like them soft and sweet."

"And you don't care if they're married," Declan jabbed.

"Hey, if a woman wants a piece of this," he held his arms out to signify his normal physique, "who am I to deny her? Some women aren't happily married. If they show some interest, why deny them some pleasure?"

"I can't believe you really think that way."

"No one is perfect, Dec." Vaughn wrinkled his nose. "And that's what happened to your marriage, huh?"

"Don't want to talk about it."

"I'm sorry, man."

"There are a lot of men out there with your philosophy. I don't happen to buy into it."

Declan shook his head, irritated at the subject of the conversation. "I need a drink, a hot shower, a pair of sweat pants which you've only worn with underwear, and a place to sleep."

"I can accommodate most of that. I can't promise you that I've worn underwear with all my sweat pants and lounge pants."

"Great."

"Grow up," Vaughn scoffed. "I am a good enough friend to have gone out and bought you some boxers, a pair of lounge pants, a pair of jeans, and a T-shirt. And lucky for you, this house has two full baths, so you can use the one just off the hallway and get that shower you asked for. There's some travel soaps and stuff that I swiped from hotels. Clean towels too."

"You're a solid best friend," Declan praised as he rested a hand on Vaughn's shoulder.

"I'm so sorry all this happened, Dec. I loved Stacy. She was a really great woman."

"I didn't realize you still kept in touch."

"You've been gone a long time. The rest of us live here. We interact," he confirmed as he moved to the kitchen and opened a cupboard where a half-empty bottle of Jack sat.

Vaughn pulled it down, then retrieved two glasses from another cupboard. He poured them each two fingers of the liquid, and then handed Declan a glass.

"To Stacy," he toasted.

Declan couldn't find the words to reciprocate, so he simply saluted and drank down the amber liquid.

After a hot shower, Declan retreated to the spare room in Vaughn's tiny house. He assumed it was usually used as an office of some kind. On the walls were sports posters and jerseys from multiple sports and teams. It was as if Vaughn couldn't pick a favorite.

Declan would have thought he'd have been a big baseball fan, as that was what they played when they were younger. But as Vaughn and Lacy had both pointed out, Declan had been gone for a very long time.

There was a small TV on a dresser, a computer, and a desk full of papers which Vaughn must have hurried and stacked together upon Declan's notice of arrival. The room had a futon, which Vaughn had made up into a bed before Declan had arrived. The carpet also looked as though he'd quickly run a vacuum over it.

The gesture was sweet and appreciated.

Declan plugged in his phone and let it charge for a few minutes. When the screen turned on, he began to check his messages from the day.

It was now twelve-thirty and he wondered why he'd turned on the damn phone. There were messages from clients, co-workers, and one from Lacy he'd never received since he'd been on the airplane at the time.

He sorted through text messages from people offering condolences. Word had spread fast, he thought.

Another half hour, and he sorted through emails and shuffled a few off to his assistant.

By one o'clock, he'd given up on caring who needed anything from him. They were going to release his mother in a few hours, and he promised he'd be there to pick her up and take her home. He was sure that they would release his sister's body to the mortuary today, and that would be something else they'd have to attend to—planning a funeral.

Declan reached across to the small table where the lamp was, and set his phone down. Reaching up, he turned off the light.

⚜

LACY CLOSED HER LAPTOP AND SET IT ON HER NIGHTSTAND. She'd made it a rule, a long time ago, not to take work to bed with her, but with this case, she just couldn't help herself. Later in the morning, when they had their briefing meeting, it would be brought up that there were similarities to another recent murder and perhaps they could look at that to focus on leads—of which they had none. Had her captain not kicked her out of the building, she'd still have been there working on the case. Stacy needed justice and the clock was ticking.

Laying back against her headboard she thought about talking to Stacy the day before she died. They had plans for drinks on Friday night. Just a quick glass of wine. Lacy wanted to know how Toby's assignment turned out after he'd interviewed her.

She supposed she could ask Tom. After all, later that day they'd be questioning him, again.

Pressing a hand to her stomach, she thought of the afternoon when the police came to the house to question her father in her mother's death. He'd dismissed her to the other room, but she'd stood outside the door and listened.

There were two officers who came to the house that cold

November morning. She'd remember them in time as a good cop and a bad cop. Now she understood that.

The woman had coddled her father. She spoke softly, made sure he was comfortable, and even made sure he had something to drink. When she asked a question, it was soft and understanding.

The man was completely different. He paced the room, looking at everything from a distance. When he asked a question, it was loud and he'd step toward her father in a manner that said he questioned every answer her father gave.

She understood the contrast now, and she used the same tactics in her own job. Sometimes the confession came when the suspect least expected a change in questions or attitude. Already, she knew she'd be using the same line of questioning on Tom. Even if he didn't kill his wife, he might know something he didn't even know he knew.

Lacy turned out the light, closed her eyes, and tried to rest her mind. But her mind wouldn't calm. Images of Stacy would disturb her. Thoughts of what might have happened to her popped into her mind. And then there was Declan.

The look on his face when she'd apologized had been one of absolute surprise. She'd held in the apology for years. It had all been part of her therapy, to apologize to those she had hurt. And she'd hurt a lot of people over the years. The trauma of losing her mother at such a young age in such a devastating way had caused her to lash out. She was the epitome of sex, drugs, and rock n' roll. What that must have done to her already broken father— well, she hated to think about it.

She'd been completely serious when she told Declan to get the kids into counseling right away. The thought that they might go down the same path she had, well it broke her heart.

Lacy flipped over onto her side. Pounding the pillow under her head into a more comfortable shape, she closed her eyes. Stacy's image was soon there again, and now she decided she'd just have to sleep with it. Perhaps what bothered her most was the fact that she, too, ran on that same trail three times a week. Was this random? Could it just as easily have been she, herself who had been murdered?

She tried to change the image in her head again. If she had to think of that log in the woods, then she wanted a much nicer image. Squeezing her eyes tighter, she thought about the night that Declan took her out to that very spot. He promised it was very exclusive. Only a few people knew about it. Somehow, she'd let him seduce her until it was comfortable to walk back to his car in the parking lot—and the rest was history.

Oh, but she'd really liked him. He probably didn't know that because she'd turned into some kind of lunatic when he was around after that. She might have even accused him once of taking advantage of her, but that wasn't true. Nothing could have been farther from the truth. It was fact that Declan Matthews never left her mind, or her heart, and that had been a problem.

Her eyes popped open and she sat up in bed. It was well after one o'clock and it was obvious she wasn't going to get any sleep.

Kicking her legs over the edge of the bed, she pulled her fingers through her hair. Maybe a warm bath would help. Her partner, Carl, had given her a gift basket from Bath and Body Works for her birthday in June. She knew he'd been in a fix over it. What did a married man buy another woman, other than his wife, for her birthday? It was the best he could have done. To be honest, she'd have been happier with a Starbucks card or one for a pizza place. But the basket sat on the back of her toilet, as some kind of decoration, unopened. Maybe it was time to pull out the bath salts. What would it hurt?

Lacy closed the door to the bathroom, and pulled off the wrap on the basket. She'd never even looked at what was inside the basket. Candles, bath salts, lotion, and a loofah. She chuckled to herself as the scents hit her nose. "What the hell made him think I liked roses?"

With a twist of the faucet, she began to fill the bathtub. She opened the bath salts, read the instructions, and then poured the entire pouch into the water. Rose fragrance filled her nose and she coughed.

Reaching into the medicine cabinet, she found a lighter and lit the candle. Setting it on the edge of the tub, she then stepped out of her pajamas and into the warm, scented water.

Lacy let out a long, deep moan as she slid into the water. Okay, so maybe women did have this figured out. There was something to the soft, floral water that enveloped her. The flicker of the candle was mesmerizing.

Had the scent only been invigorating, she could climb out of the tub and head back to work. As it was, she was now fighting to keep her eyes open.

When the water began to cool, Lacy pulled the plug, and stepped out of the tub. She wrapped herself in the only plush thing she owned—her robe.

Instead of heading back to bed, she walked out to the living room, gathered up a quilt, and went to lay on the couch. It worked when she was sick, had cramps, or her friend from the academy came to visit and took her bedroom. Surely, it would work for a restless night so she could get just a few hours of sleep.

Lacy wrapped herself up in the quilt and closed her eyes. Soon the chill was gone and she was warm and comfortable. She still fought for sleep, but now Stacy wasn't haunting her dreams—Stacy's brother was.

6

Declan bolted out of slumber and straight up when his cell phone rang. Dear God, hadn't he turned that damn thing off?

He fumbled for it in the dim light of morning. When he had it in his hand, he strained his eyes to read the caller ID.

Letting out a deep groan, he answered. "Matthews here."

"Did I wake you? Oh, Declan, I'm so sorry," his assistant Angie apologized. "I had a few calls come in this morning and I knew you'd want to know about them."

Declan fell back on the futon, which had been more comfortable than he'd have imagined. "Whatcha got, Ange?"

He listened as she rattled on about meetings that other firms wanted to have with him over client settlements. Trying to wrap his brain around a few of the items, he directed her to pass them on to other associates.

"And your ex-wife's lawyer called again. They don't want to settle on the amount you offered."

It was too freaking early for a headache, he thought. "She shouldn't be asking for more. That's what divorce is all about," he muttered under his breath. "I'll deal with that later. Why don't you call them back and tell them where I am. Tell them exactly why I'm where I am," he let it be the growl he felt in his chest.

"Oh, Declan. I'm so sorry for your loss. I just can't imagine."

One of the things he loved about Angie was that she never became insulted by his quick anger. She kept her composure even when he couldn't.

"Tell Charles I'll be calling him. I'm going to need a short leave of absence. It looks like I'm going to be here for quite a while. There's so much to do," he admitted as much to himself as he was telling Angie. "I might need a personal favor, Ange."

"Anything."

"I left the office yesterday and flew straight here. I'm currently sleeping on a friend's futon in a pair of sweat pants he bought me at Walmart." He heard her snicker. "I'm going to need one of my suits, and I sure could use some of my own clothes."

"Consider it done. How do I get into your fancy condo?"

He explained that he kept an extra key in his office in a desk drawer, hidden in an envelope, in a date book.

Then, after they hung up, he texted her a list of the items he would like her to ship to him. It sucked that he'd have to pay to have his favorite suit shipped to him, but his sister deserved at least that.

Seated on the edge of the futon, Declan ran his hands over his hair. He was exhausted clear to his bones. He wasn't sure there was enough coffee in the world to keep him awake. But the aroma of it helped.

After a trip to the bathroom, and some cold water scrubbed over his face, Declan walked out to the kitchen where a sweaty Vaughn stood leaned over the sink, staring out the window.

"Hey, man. You have enough coffee for two?" he asked, and he could have sworn Vaughn wiped his eyes before turning around. Surely sweat had dripped from his hair. Vaughn wasn't the kind of man to be crying over anything.

"Yeah. I need it to kick me in the ass today," Vaughn said as he moved to the cupboard for two cups.

"You've already been out for a run? What the hell time is it?"

"Six. I don't usually go till later, but I couldn't sleep." He poured each of them a cup of coffee then motioned to the small kitchen table as an invitation for him to sit.

Declan took a seat and looked at the scattered items on the table. Phone bill. Few receipts. Forgotten cup from Starbucks. He picked up the large Ziploc bag of chocolate chip cookies. "Baking?"

Vaughn's eyes went wide, then perhaps a little misty. "Gift from a friend. You know I can't bake."

Declan forced a chuckle as Vaughn sat down next to him.

"So why are you up so early?"

"Figure I'll go in to the office early today and then if you need anything, I'm here for you. I know today is going to be hard."

"Tell me about it. Mom will be out of the hospital in a few hours. They got her calm and hydrated. Dad stayed too, and though not a patient, they took care of him."

"What about Tom?"

"I'm supposing Mom will want to go right over. His parents are there taking care of him. You know how Janice is about mothering, so she's right in her element. She had the kids calm, and that alone was probably a huge help. I'll help him sort through things today."

Vaughn rubbed his eyes. "I ran through there today. Through the wooded area. I swear you could feel her. I swear you could feel both of them."

"Both? What the hell does that mean?"

Vaughn sat back in his chair with his mug between his hands. "Carley Francess-Hastings."

"What about her? And didn't you have a thing with her?"

Vaughn nodded slowly. "Yeah. Old news. But she was killed

near there about two months ago or so. Broken neck. They said she fell and rolled down a hill."

"There aren't many hills around there."

"No, there aren't. Makes you wonder."

"I think a kid at Starbucks told me about her. Or mentioned that there had been someone else." Declan sipped his coffee. "I talked to my assistant this morning. She's shipping some of my things. Something tells me I'll be a bit before I'm home and back to work."

"Lacy will get this asshole. Don't worry. It won't be long."

"Did she get Carley's asshole?"

Vaughn shook his head. "No."

"I'll wait it out then." Declan stood, poured the cold remnants of his coffee down the sink, then rinsed his cup before turning to Vaughn. "Thank you for putting me up last night and for the clothes. I'll pay you back."

"No need, man. Least I could do."

"I'm sure I'll be staying at my parents' house tonight. I'll let you know if that's not the case."

Vaughn laughed. "As if they'd turn their prodigal son away."

Declan gave him a humored nod and started back to the spare room. But something had him stopping and looking back at the man sitting at the kitchen table. The humor had gone now. His head was bowed and his hands cupped his coffee mug. He looked broken—sad. Perhaps Vaughn had been right. Declan had been the one that had left, the rest of those he knew and loved still lived in the same town they'd grown up in. Why wouldn't they all be upset about his sister's death?

AFTER PICKING HIS PARENTS UP FROM THE HOSPITAL, HE TOOK them back home. He wasn't sure what it was that they'd given to his mother, but her nerves were calmer, and her voice was stronger.

She talked from the moment he'd entered her room at the hospital until he got them settled into their house. His father never said a word.

They were only home a few moments when Mrs. Clancy showed up with an armful of food.

"Oh, Declan, I just heard. I would have been over here yesterday, but I just heard. How's your mama? She must be a wreck. And look at you all grown up and so handsome. I've heard you're a very successful lawyer in New York. I'm sorry you had to come home to this. I made them meals," she said with a shake of her head. "And listen to me. I'm nervous, and I'm sad, oh, so sad." He saw the tears welling in her eyes.

"Let me take those from you, Mrs. Clancy. Come on in."

"Oh, thank you, Declan."

He stepped back and let the older woman, who'd been an older woman since he'd been young, pass by him. When his mother came to see who was there, she fell into Mrs. Clancy's open embrace and sobbed.

Declan remembered that Mrs. Clancy was a school nurse, back when. She had a gracious way about her, and her caring nature was comforting.

Draping an arm over Declan's mother, she escorted her back to the living room.

Declan lifted his foot to kick closed the door when he noticed Lacy and another man walking up the front walk.

"Hey, Matthews," she called out to him.

"Lacy."

"This is Detective Carl Moss."

"Sir," Declan said with a nod of his head. "I have to set these dinners in the kitchen. Come on in, I'll be right with you."

"We can help you with that," she said, reaching out and taking one of the serving platters, and Carl another. "Kitchen back this way?" she asked as she walked down the hallway.

"To your left," he directed, as he closed the door and he and Carl followed.

As they all walked through the door to the kitchen, he realized Lacy had never been to his house, at least not when he'd lived there. Of course, his relationship with her was short lived. A few movies, dinners, and rolls in the back seat of his car didn't make much of a relationship. He'd never known much about her, really.

Declan took the meals and put them into the already full refrigerator. "Looks like they've had a few visitors."

"People around here feel like a meal gives comfort," she said.

He agreed with a nod, managed the meals into the refrigerator, and turned back to them as he closed the door.

"I assume you're here to talk to my parents?"

Carl, his hands in his pockets, rocked back on his heels. "No, we're here to talk to you."

"Me? Okay. I think Mrs. Clancy will keep my mother busy for a bit. Can I offer you something to drink?"

Lacy stepped toward him. "I don't think we should talk to you here. I don't want to upset your parents. Are they stable enough to be here?"

"None of us are, Lace... Lacy," he corrected when he noticed her flinch. "Mrs. Clancy is with my mom now and I'm sure she'll be sticking around. We can go out back."

Carl dipped his head in a nod. "Yep, that'll be fine," he said as he moved to the back door and opened it.

Declan exchanged a glance with Lacy before they both followed Carl outside.

He closed the door behind them and walked the detectives to the back of the yard. If they didn't want to upset his parents, then he didn't want his parents to accidentally hear them.

Lacy tucked her hair behind her ear. "You stayed with Vaughn Price last night?"

"Yeah. Mom and Dad were at the hospital. He bought me clothes at Walmart since I'd flown straight here from the office."

Lacy took a long look at him. "Looks like that's what you were wearing yesterday."

"Let's just say he bought me something to relax in. I'm having clothes sent out," Declan explained.

Carl crossed his arms in front of him. Declan assumed it was to make himself look bigger, as he was a lanky man. He probably stood six-foot-four, and had a narrow build. If he wanted to look menacing, like Lacy did, he had to work on it.

"How well do you know Mr. Price?" Carl asked, his voice low like a growl.

"I've known him since we were in the first grade. We've been friends ever since."

"Before your sister's death, when was the last time you'd spoken to Mr. Price?"

Declan crossed his arms in front of him, mimicking Carl's stance. "I don't see what this has to do with Stacy."

Lacy, who shifted a glance between the two of them in their obvious fight for male dominance, pursed her lips. "It's relevant."

Declan dragged a hand through his hair and thought. "It had been a while I guess. Maybe a year or two."

"But you fell right back in line, huh?" Carl continued his questioning.

"You can do that with some people. Others not so much," he replied, fighting the urge to look directly at Lacy.

Lacy tucked her hair behind her ear again. "Did he talk to you about any of his relationships since you've been back? Or did you know about any of them in the past?"

Now Declan understood the questioning. He tucked his hands into the pockets of his suit pants. "I heard about the other girl that died."

"Yeah," Lacy agreed. "Did he ever tell you about her?"

Declan felt the prickling of deceit rise up his spine. He ran his tongue over his teeth as he gave thought to what it was she was trying to pull out of him. "Carley Francess was someone who was a few years younger than we were in school. Younger than Stacy, too. I didn't know her, really."

She nodded, then narrowed her dark eyes and locked them with his. "Let's get this right out in the open, Matthews. Did Vaughn ever talk about having a relationship with the woman?"

That prickling of his spine was quickly going to turn into a cold sweat if he didn't reel it in. But he was a damn good lawyer. This was a feeling he'd learned to control years ago. No one, not even Lacy Pratt, was going to see him buckle.

"No man is made of stone, Detective Pratt," he added with a little bite of his own. "Yes. I know Carley was married. And I know that Vaughn had something going on with her. I don't know the extent of it. I don't know if her husband ever found out. I don't know how long it had been going on. He likes married women, or they like him," he corrected. "I do know that he was shaken up this morning, though he was trying not to let me see it. I'd have to assume it was because my sister's death hit too close to home. One, it was my sister, and like you, he reminded me that I'm the one that left and the rest of you carried on intertwined in each other's lives. But I think it brought back some feelings about Carley's death as well."

"She was killed only thirty feet from where your sister was found," Lacy informed him. "Two and a half months ago."

Declan nodded. "I'd heard that too." Now he narrowed his gaze on Lacy. "I heard she broke her neck, or something like that. However, it seems to be a thought that she was killed. I heard you never caught her killer. I'd have to assume by now you ruled out Vaughn, so why all the questions?"

Carl stuck a finger in his ear, wiggled it around as if it would make him hear better. "We have reason to believe that Vaughn and..."

Lacy held up a hand. "We just needed to ask," she said, cutting Carl off from his explanation. "They'll be releasing your sister today to the funeral home."

"We have a meeting with them at three. Tom is coming over in an hour to discuss plans with me and my parents. His parents are keeping the kids and doing a fine job, I might add."

"We're headed over there now. We need to ask him some questions, get his alibi again."

"You think he had something to do with this?"

"No," she said firmly. "I don't think he does. But until I have a lead of any kind, I'm not ruling anyone out. Not even you."

"You know where I was. I have plane tickets and an office full of people in New York that know where I was."

Her lips curled into a slight smile. "I have two murders I'm working on, Matthews. I don't know where you were two months ago." She turned and started for the gate on the side of the house. "I'll be in touch, Matthews," she called back as she walked through the gate to the front yard.

Declan looked over at Carl, who stood nearly dumbfounded at his partner's exit.

"I guess she's done here," Declan acknowledged and Carl gave him a slow nod.

"Guess we'll be in touch."

On his long legs, Carl strolled out of the yard, following his partner.

Declan stood alone in the back yard until he heard her car drive away. He rubbed his eyes, which stung from the lack of sleep. What in the hell did they want with Vaughn? There was no way he had anything to do with Carley's death, no matter what his relationship with her was. And why ask about that now, especially when Stacy's murder was on the front burner?

The back door opened and Mrs. Clancy poked her head out. "Declan, your mama wants her slippers from her room. I don't want to go prying around. Would you mind getting them?"

He nodded. "I'll be right in," he said and Mrs. Clancy ducked back into the house.

He wanted this nightmare to be over, he thought as he walked back toward the house. He wanted his normal life back. The one where he fought for others and argued over their problems and shortcomings in life. What he wouldn't give to be all alone in his condo wishing he were surrounded by friends. Instead, he was surrounded by friends, and because of the circumstances, he was miserable.

He needed little reminding that this wasn't about him. This was about his sister and the many lives she held together. Until everything was settled, he'd be there to honor her. And if Detective Lacy Pratt didn't find his sister's killer, Declan would. Then he might need himself a lawyer.

7

Lacy could feel Carl's eyes steady on her as she drove out of the neighborhood and toward Tom's house.

"Got a problem, Moss?" she asked without shifting a look at him.

"You stopped me back there from telling him what we know. Why?"

"He didn't need to know it," she answered flatly.

"We have a possible serial killer on our hands, and we think we might know who he is, and we can't tell him to watch his back?"

She turned and headed down the street lined with businesses she'd watched crop up over the years, and then some would shut down. What she wouldn't give for a cup of coffee right about now.

It just so happened that she knew Tom liked the coffee at Griff's Donuts, so she pulled over and parked the car.

"Listen, Moss. We have no evidence against Vaughn Price, except that he likes married women. And as Declan said, they like him, too."

"And Stacy Watts was one of those women," he reminded her and she flinched at it.

"She was."

It sickened her to think that Stacy had been having an affair with Declan's old pal. But she had. Lacy felt a bit cheated too.

Why in the hell would someone like Stacy need a lover? Why was her life not good enough with a doting husband and two amazing kids at home? Why in God's name did she have to sneak around with a man who collected married women as trophies? What could Vaughn Price possibly have in his pants that no woman could get at home?

"You okay?" Carl asked as she hadn't moved to get out of the car.

"Yeah. Tom Watts happens to like the coffee here. I forgot to eat. He also likes the jelly-filled donuts and I could use one too."

Carl gave her a nod. "I'll go get a bag, and a couple of coffees. I see you're going to try and make him feel at ease. That's kind of you. Just don't let your heart get in the way, Lace."

She shot him a look when he shortened her name. "My heart is just fine."

"Yeah, well you ran with Stacy. You knew her from childhood. You knew her brother, and Vaughn too. I think this is a bit personal."

It might have been, but she wasn't going to let that interfere. "I'm fine. I'll get the job done, and soon, too."

"Take a minute and breathe. I'll be right back."

Carl unfolded himself from the car and went inside the store. Lacy stayed back and did as he told her to do—breathe.

Breathing didn't come easy though. She was sickened by it all.

There were so many layers to this mystery now, and it all brought back old memories—old fears.

Her mother had been killed nearly twenty-one years earlier in a similar pattern. Lacy hadn't learned about her own mother's affair until much later. It sickened her now to think about it.

Like Tom, Lacy's father had been a doting man. What had made her mother want to be with someone else?

It still hurt to think she'd been betraying them. And to think, she could never ask her why. It was a big part of why Lacy hadn't ever wanted to get married. Of course, the right man had never come along, but if he did, would she be loyal? Obviously it wasn't in her blood to be.

Carl came back to the car with three coffees and a bag of donuts. He handed her the coffee tray to hold while he managed into the car and buckled his belt.

"Compliments of Pastor Ralph," he said, as the pastor walked out the door and toward the car.

Lacy rolled down her window. "Thank you for the coffees and the donuts. I appreciate it."

"My pleasure. Carl says you're headed over to Tom Watts' house."

"Yes, sir," she confirmed.

"I'm meeting with the family this afternoon at three. Horrible thing that's happened to them." He reached into the car and patted her shoulder. "I'm praying for them, and for all of you. Be safe."

Pastor Ralph walked away and she watched as he climbed into an old Chrysler, probably as old as the church that gave him the car to drive. It was sad, really. A man who baptized, wedded, and buried the people of the town, and his car could hardly pass emissions. Someone should do something about that, she thought.

But as she wasn't a big candidate for a parishioner, having given up on God at the age of twelve, she didn't see where she should get involved. The people in town loved the man, and they went to him with their problems, confessions, and whatnot. She'd give him the respect he deserved, she just didn't have to buy into his greater good.

There was evil in the world, and she'd made it her mission to fight it. So she would do just that and be grateful that one of God's servants bought her a donut and a cup of coffee.

When she pulled up in front of Tom and Stacy's house, she put the car in park, and let the engine idle for a moment.

"Seriously, Pratt. Let me go in and you stay here. This is too close to you," Carl wiped crumbs from his shirt.

"Like hell. You'll march right in there and tell that man his wife was cheating on him. I'm not going to let you do that."

"It's part of our investigation."

"Yeah, and when she's been buried, and we know more, you can tell him."

"Take your time then," he offered. "When you're ready."

"I'm ready."

She pushed open the door and stepped out into the street. As they walked up the front step, the door opened, and a version of Tom she'd never seen stood in the doorway.

His curly hair was obviously tousled from his fingers having been in it all night. Dark circles shadowed his eyes. His cheeks were hollow as if he hadn't eaten since yesterday, but with his mother there, she was sure he'd been fed.

"I was expecting you," he said as he held the door open to them. "My folks just took the kids out for a bit. I knew you'd be coming by."

"Sorry to have to do this, Tom," Lacy said. "I'm so sorry for your loss, too."

"Thanks."

They stepped past him and into the house. Carl, as usual, kept his keen eye on everything. He was good that way. He saw things that most people would assume were ordinary, but he knew if it was out of place.

"Where do we need to sit?" Tom asked, lost in his own home.

"Where are you most comfortable?" Lacy asked. "I know you like Griff's coffee. So we stopped and got you one. A donut too. Actually Pastor Ralph bought them."

"He's a good guy. Let's go to the kitchen."

They followed him to the kitchen. It certainly had a woman's touch—his mother's. She'd seen what chaos and grief did to a man with children. Sadly, she'd seen it much too often.

Nothing was out of place here though, and everything wiped clean.

Tom sat down at the kitchen table. Lacy and Carl followed suit. She leaned in on her arms, comforting. Carl leaned back in his chair, legs extended out, more casual—observant.

"Tom, we're here trying to learn anything we can to find out who did this," she said and he nodded. "Can you tell us if she had any problems with anyone? Has anyone threatened her? Anything you can think of is helpful."

He shook his head. "I can't think of anyone. Everyone loved her."

"Tell us about her past few days. What was she doing? Planning?"

Tom pushed his hands into his mat of curls, resting his elbows on the table. "She had a shift at the coffee shop. A PTA meeting. She'd made chocolate chip cookies for it." He took a deep breath. "Every day she'd run that trail," he said as a sob choked him up and Lacy rested a hand on his shoulder.

"Take your time."

Tom sniffed. "Sorry."

"Don't be. Just breathe and take a moment."

Tom wiped away his tears, then rubbed his hands on his pants. "She'd go for a run, usually an hour, sometimes two."

Lacy exchanged a look with Carl, but he kept quiet.

"Was she always running during that time?"

Tom lifted his head, a deep crease between his brows. "She said she was. She'd park in the lot, where she'd parked yesterday. Where else would she be?"

"Just asking," she said. "Tell me about her friends at the coffee shop."

Tom rubbed at his eyes. "You're her friend."

Lacy smiled. "I am. That's why I want to get to the bottom of this right away."

He nodded. "She enjoyed spending time with you. I know you

and Declan dated, and she thought that was awkward at first, but..."

She caught Carl's sideways glance. Yeah, she'd have to explain that too, she supposed.

"We were good. Declan was a quick phase. Did she spend time with anyone at the store? Anyone in particular?"

He shook his head. "People come and go. She was sort of like the mother figure I suppose. People looked up to her." Tom rubbed his hand over the back of his neck. "I'm sick over this."

"I am too."

He looked up at her, locked eyes with her. "They said you'd give me details. I haven't seen her yet. I know Declan has, but..." He sucked in a sharp breath. "Is she bad? Did he rape her? Beat her?" Tom could hardly say the words before he broke down.

Lacy reached for his hands and grasped them in hers. This was beyond good cop, and she could see Carl itching to jump in, but he refrained.

She understood them leaving it to her to tell him the details. But she didn't much care about having to do so. "She was not raped."

He lifted his eyes to hers. "She wasn't?" There was a hope that filled his voice. It was a false hope, but she understood it. It was at least something to know that wasn't the reason someone had killed the person you loved.

Lacy shook her head. "No. She wasn't raped. In fact, we believe she was killed by someone she was comfortable with. Someone she knew."

"Why?"

"Because it's evident that she trusted her killer, Tom. She had a few bruises, signs that there might have been a slight struggle, but nothing as if she were warding off a full-on attack. She was strangled."

That had the man nearly hyperventilating, even though he'd already been told that much, she knew.

She rested a hand on his back until his breathing calmed. "Whoever left her there wanted her to look peaceful. They laid her on that log, tidied her clothes, and even left a flower next to her."

"Maybe it was some kind of accident. Maybe someone found her and laid her there."

Lacy shook her head. She understood wanting that to be the truth too.

"I'm going to get you some answers. We're going to bring in the person responsible for this."

He wiped at his eyes, and lifted them to meet hers. "That other woman that was murdered a few months ago. They found her in the same place."

"Almost. She was near the creek on an adjoining path."

"Did they find who did that to her?"

Lacy shook her head. "They are very similar and we're hoping that if it were the same person, they'll have made a mistake with this. I'm not used to not getting my guy, Tom. Whoever did this will pay. I swear it."

"I believe you," he said with a sniff.

"Are you okay here alone? Can I call someone for you?" she offered just as the doorbell rang.

He blinked his eyes quickly. "That'll be Declan. He was going to pick me up."

"He didn't mention that when I spoke to him," she said.

"I called him right before you got here. I just think it would be best if I didn't drive."

"Good thinking." She turned to Carl. "Why don't you finish your coffee with Tom. Have another donut. I'm going to talk to Declan for a moment," she said, giving Carl a look that hopefully stated she didn't want him near her when she talked to him.

Lacy walked to the door and pulled it open.

"Making your rounds, Detective Pratt?" he asked.

"I am. He said he called you for a ride."

"He did. He didn't think he was stable enough to drive."

"Smart guy," she said stepping out onto the porch and shutting the door behind her. "Is there anything I or the department can do for you to help get her memorial set up?"

Declan studied her. "Is this a regular thing the police department does?"

"Let me rephrase. Is there anything I can do for you all? As a friend of Stacy's? As an old friend of yours?" She swallowed hard when she said it. Having him home had unraveled her a bit. It was easy to be Stacy's friend and to forget that she was Declan's sister. But seeing him, having had drinks with him, just talking to him—it was stirring up a lot of old feelings.

He must have read that in her questioning too, as he stepped in closer to her, enough so she could smell the soap he'd used that morning. "That's a nice offer. You could catch her killer."

"That I will do as the detective."

"But the woman is offering her assistance."

"It's not so strange, Matthews."

"I'm sure my family would consider anything helpful. I don't know what I could possibly ask for specifically." He reached his hand to her arm and gave it a slight rub which had her skin growing warm. "On a personal level, I'd like to ask for you to go to dinner with me, maybe after the funeral."

"You're asking me out?"

"I'm asking you to share a meal with me. I'm going to need to separate from my family for an hour, and it would be nice to do it with an old friend."

Old friend. She'd take that title. "I'd like that. Are you staying with Vaughn tonight?"

He shook his head. "No. I'll be staying with my parents tonight."

"I assume he went to work this morning?"

Declan crossed his arms in front of him. "This sounds like a line of questioning."

"Just filling in some holes, Matthews."

"Yeah, he got up early and went for a run. He wanted to get to work early so he could be with my family if we needed anything. That's what friends do, Pratt," he sharply pronounced her name.

She wondered if he'd feel the same way when word came out about his sister's affair with the deemed friend.

"Tom's inside waiting for you. We'll be in touch if we have anything new," she said as Carl opened the front door.

Declan gave her a nod and passed into the house.

Carl descended the stairs as Lacy slid her sunglasses on, and Carl followed suit.

"Where to now?" he asked as they each opened their car doors and slid inside.

"I think it's time we talk to Vaughn. Declan said he went to work early so he could be home early. I think I'd like to catch him there."

"At home?"

"Yep. I'd like to get inside the house so you can do your expert eye scan," she said shooting him a grin as she started the car and pulled away from the curb.

❧ 8 ❧

Declan served coffee, helped sort through papers, opened tissue boxes, and listened to his mother and brother-in-law sob as Pastor Ralph helped to console them and make the arrangements for Stacy's funeral.

They were starting from scratch. She had life insurance, but at thirty-two, planning her own funeral hadn't been first on her mind. It would become their choice as to what to do with her body.

Their mother wanted her dressed in a nice dress, in a fancy casket, with sprays of flowers for her baby girl. Tom had enough information to know that his wife wanted to be cremated and scattered in very special places. He'd lost his composure and removed himself from the kitchen table when he told them she had once mentioned that she'd wanted to be scattered at the log in the wooded area, but that wasn't an option since that's where they'd found her body. Who would have ever guessed that a childhood play spot would become an area of death?

Declan followed Tom to the back porch where he found him gripping the porch railing and sobbing.

"Man, you okay?"

Tom shook his head. "My heart hurts so bad that I'm afraid that it's going to burst. I keep thinking it's all a bad dream, and I'm going to wake up and it'll all be over. I'm all my kids have now."

Declan rested his hand on Tom's back. "You all have a lot of support. Mom and Dad. Your folks. And I'm not going anywhere for a while."

"I appreciate it all. I really do." He turned toward Declan. "But we will have to go on at some point."

"And we will all make sure you're ready for that." Declan rested his back against the railing. "You know that Lacy went through this as a child."

Tom lifted his eyes to him. "Through what?"

"Her mother was killed by someone," he said, thinking it sounded less horrible than using the word *murdered*. "I think she was twelve or fourteen. I'm not sure."

"What the hell is wrong with people?"

"She wanted me to make sure the kids got counseling. She knows what she went through and how she dealt with it as a teenager and into adulthood. It's why she does what she does."

"I had no idea about that." Tom blew out a breath. "I'll do that for the kids."

"Good. You should do it for yourself too. I'm going to make Mom and Dad see someone when they can. And if finance is ever an issue for it, I'll take care of it," he promised.

"I appreciate that." Tom turned and leaned his back against the rail as Declan had. "Whoever killed her didn't rape her. I have that little bit of comfort in this whole thing. It doesn't make me understand it any more than that, but it helps."

"How do you know that?"

"Lacy told me."

It seemed so odd that someone would kill to just kill and not take something for themselves. He certainly didn't have a murderous thought process, but he'd read enough books, and been a lawyer long enough. And he'd seen his sister. Minus the few bruises, she looked peaceful.

"Why don't we go back inside. We're going to have to plow through all of this," Declan said as he stood upright from the rail.

"I just want to make it go away," Tom admitted as he too stood and moved from the railing. "Thank you for being here. You're a rock, and this can't be easy on you, either."

"I'll crack when it's over. Seems to be the way I work. It's what makes me a good lawyer." He rested a hand on Tom's shoulder. "Is there anything I can help you with in there? Anything you want to say that you might be holding back?"

"Not yet. Thanks for that. I'll let you know. Do you think your mom will be okay?"

"They'll be fine. It's going to take a long time, and it's going to take you and the kids to help them. But they'll be there for you. Make sure you let them be."

"I wouldn't have it any other way."

An hour later, the arrangements had been made for the funeral. Declan's mother retreated to her bedroom to rest, and his father to his chair. Mrs. Clancy came with her crocheting to sit on the couch, to sit with his father while Declan took Tom home.

"I don't know what I'll do when my parents go back home," Tom admitted as they pulled up in front of the house and parked behind their car.

"We'll all still be here for you."

"I've always been grateful that I married into your family."

Declan watched a broken man climb from his car and walk up the front steps of his house. How were they all going to put this behind them?

He could feel that crack in him that he said would come. Not yet, he warned himself. When his sister had been buried, and his parents returned to something normal, then maybe a bit. When his brother-in-law returned to work, and the children returned to school and to their friends, then he'd fall apart.

Until all of that happened, he'd let that sharp ache reside in his chest.

⚜

Lacy and Carl sat out front of Vaughn's house and waited. They'd been there for forty minutes already, and she could tell that Carl was getting antsy.

"So you and Matthews, huh?"

She knew he'd have to latch on to that at some point. "Yeah, so what?"

"Kinda personal then."

"It's not a huge city. It's all personal."

He gave her a nod. "Sure. So how hot was this thing you and Declan had?"

"Hot enough. Young enough. Dumb enough to forget and move on, Moss."

"Got it." He scanned the street again. "I don't think he's coming back this way."

"He will," she said slowly as she watched his car turn onto the street. "I told you. Right on time."

Vaughn sped down the street and right into his driveway. She could have certainly gotten him on speeding, but she'd let it slide. She was fairly sure she was about to make one more connection that would close the gap on deeming him the killer of Carley Francess-Hastings and Stacy Watts.

They both climbed from the car as Vaughn rounded his and headed toward his front door. When he saw them, he turned around.

"Hey, Lace. Carl."

"Can we talk to you a few minutes?" she asked, as he looked at his keys to find the right one for the door.

"Um, sure," he said looking up at her. "I was going to change and head toward Declan's."

"It'll only take a few minutes. If you have a Coke, I'd love one."

He nodded. "Sure. Come on in."

Ah, the invite. She loved it when it worked right. And asking him for a Coke got them all the way into the kitchen and off the front porch and out of the front hallway.

She and Carl followed Vaughn to the kitchen. "Have a seat," he offered as he went to the refrigerator and pulled out three Cokes. "I have a weakness for soft drinks. I run miles and miles a week just to get them out of my system. I'm not sure how to break my habit."

He set the drinks down in front of them and then took a seat.

Carl picked up a bag of chocolate chip cookies which sat on the table. "Been baking?"

Vaughn shook his head. "Not me. They were a gift."

A gift from Stacy, she thought. Hadn't Tom told them she'd been making cookies for the PTA? Looked like Vaughn had been a lucky recipient too. Not that it convicted him of anything other than having good taste in baked goods.

From the corner of her eye, she could see that Carl was casing the place with a careful eye. He was good when he was silent, and it was just how she liked him.

"I'm sure you understand, we need to ask, what were you doing at the murder scene yesterday?"

His eyes had gone wide and he quickly sipped from his Coke. "I run there. That's where I run," he repeated. "I take the trail from the parking lot to Devil's Fork. If I run longer I go all the way to the Thompson Bridge. I'd gone to run."

"Was that the first run you'd gone on yesterday?"

He blinked hard. "Sometimes I run in the morning. Today I did that. I got up early and went for a run. Depending on what kind of day I'm having, I'll go back."

"I know this is hard on you, since Declan is your friend and all."

"Yeah. I'd really like to get over there, too."

"You will. Can I have a few more minutes?"

"Of course."

Lacy folded her hands on the table. "You and Declan haven't really kept up much since he moved to New York, have you?"

Vaughn shrugged. "Here and there. A few emails. We haven't visited each other, or anything like that. If he posts a picture on Facebook, I like it. Things like that."

"Yet you were there with him yesterday."

He began to tap his fingers on the table. A nervous habit that people with something to hide were keen to do. "He called me from his office before he flew out here. He told me Stacy had been killed and that he was coming to town."

"Why call you?"

"He knew I'd be here. Ear to the ground. That kind of thing."

"So you met him at the running trail?"

"Yeah."

"And you offered him a place to stay."

"I did. I did that right away when he'd called. I figured he wouldn't want to stay with me, since his parents are here and his brother-in-law. But when he took his mom to the hospital, then he didn't want to go back to their house. I could understand that."

"Sure." Now she rubbed her palms together. It was time to pull this together a bit. "Vaughn, I know you were in a relationship with Carley Francess-Hastings."

His face went pale. Placing his hands flat on the table, he looked up at her and she was sure there was more sadness in his eyes than guilt. "God, how did you find out about that?"

"It's my job to find out things like that. Admit it, you two didn't hide it that well."

A tear streaked down his cheek and he wiped it clean. "Her husband doesn't deserve to know about it. She loved him. She just needed a little more attention."

"And you were that guy?"

"I've been that guy to a few people. I know people look down on me for that, but hey, I'm a man and when a woman is interested..."

She nodded. "I get it."

He wiped at the other tears that fell.

"Vaughn, she was found murdered not far from where Stacy was found."

He nodded and looked down at his hands. "I know."

"Okay, Vaughn. Let's talk about Stacy. We are aware that you and she were having an affair too."

"Oh, God." He lifted his hand to his mouth. "We didn't tell anyone that. How could you possibly know that?"

"Sadly, you're not the only person having affairs in this town. The first lead we had was called in from someone who knows you were here with her, in the car a few weeks ago. He didn't want to say much about it, because he too was in the parking lot with someone else's wife."

"I didn't know someone saw us," his voice was a strained whisper.

Carl moved forward now. "Lots of people saw you together. The tips we've gotten are those who run the park too. They've seen you both on the trail together."

Lacy reached her hand out to cover Vaughn's. "Is that what you meant by you run the trail twice? You run in the morning, meet your women in the afternoon?"

"God, you make me sound like a monster." He looked up at her. "I never start these things. I'm serious. The women, they come to me. I'm an easy person to talk to when their marriages are troubled."

"Why you?"

"Why not me?" He wiped his nose on his sleeve. "I'm a huge phony, I know that. But they see me at church and they come to me. I'm telling you. I've never started these things. It's just that when they're crying and they're sad..."

"You comfort them?" Carl asked.

"Yeah."

"How many married women have you helped out, Vaughn?"

"Do I have to tell you?"

Lacy sat back in the chair and shrugged. "I can tell you that I'll find out. And it'll look bad."

He let out a long slow breath. "Stacy was the fifth."

"Fifth? You've had affairs with five married women?"

"Yes."

She didn't want to sound judgmental, that wasn't why she was here. Her mother had an affair. Somewhere women just felt as though they needed this kind of comfort, she supposed. "I'm going to need their names, Vaughn."

He leaned in. "You're not going to go to them are you? I mean, some of them are happy and with their husbands. I'm not seeing all of them now. God, don't tell them I told you."

"We will handle it with kid gloves, Vaughn. I promise."

He bit down on his lip, wrung his hands, and finally looked back up at her. "Stacy, Carley, Autumn Taylor, Amy Cartwright, and Olivia Burton."

Lacy saw Carl move in, but she held up a hand to him. "Olivia Burton? Pastor Ralph Burton's wife?"

He nodded. "Yes. See what I mean? You can't go to their husbands."

"Let's just cut to the chase, Vaughn. Did you kill Stacy and Carley?"

Now his hands came to his face and the sobs grew. "No. No. No, I wouldn't do that. Dear Lord, I'd never touch them to harm them. How could you consider..."

"I have to do my job, Vaughn."

He covered his mouth. "I get it."

"Where were you when Stacy was murdered? Specifically, at four-thirty Monday afternoon?"

"I was in a meeting with potential investors. It's documented. I was at the Water Street building, in the conference room. You have to check in at security and get a badge. I did that by three. Our meeting ran from three until five."

"We have to check into it," she explained.

"Sure. Of course."

"When was the last time you saw Stacy?"

He ran his hand over his brow. "Monday morning. It wasn't our normal time. We usually met up about one-thirty. It was before she'd pick up the kids. Tom has daily meetings at that time, so she always knew he wouldn't be around." He sniffed and squeezed his eyes tight.

"Where were you when Carley Francess-Hastings was murdered?"

He was quiet for a moment, obviously thinking. "I was in Kansas City, Missouri. There was a workshop I was attending. I was supposed to fly back the night before, and we had plans to meet that morning. It snowed and they canceled my flight."

"I'll have to check that out too."

"I flew United. I always fly United. I stayed at the Marriott closest to the airport. I stayed the extra night because they canceled my flight. I even ordered room service because I just wanted to stay in my room and relax. Carley had texted me, if I remember correctly. She was fighting with her husband. I was someone to talk to."

"I'll confirm that too," Lacy said.

"I didn't hurt them, Lace. I loved them. That is my only crime. And God, don't tell Declan."

"I can't promise that I won't tell him. I might have to," she admitted. "I'll do all I can not to."

"Thanks."

Lacy and Carl both stood. "Maybe you should stay clear of

other people's wives for a bit. I'm not judging your morals, but just in case."

He nodded in agreement.

A few minutes later, Lacy and Carl were pulling away from Vaughn's house, heading back to the station.

"You believe him?" Carl asked.

"Yeah, I do. I'm still going to check out everything he told us. Line everything up."

"Who'd have expected Pastor Ralph's wife?" He let out a snort.

"You never know what's happening in someone's life that makes them stray, Moss. Pastor Ralph has a reputation to uphold, and maybe she just couldn't hold her end of that."

"It's just a bit odd that two of the five women he's had affairs with wind up dead in the same place."

"That's what's getting me. Who has it out for him?"

"You think this is linked to Vaughn?"

"It looks that way. We need to match all of this up," she said as she pulled into the Sonic drive thru.

"Needing tater tots?" He asked on a laugh.

"I think best when I have junk food."

"Yeah, that's one of the things I like best about being your partner."

9

Declan parked his car in the lot as he had the day before. Just over the small foot bridge was the trail that led to the wooded area where they'd found his sister.

He felt the stinging of tears rise in his throat, but he wasn't ready to break—not yet.

Stepping out of the car, he stood with his hand on the roof to balance himself. So many hours of his life were spent on that tree where her body had been found. The trees surrounding the area had been his playground. The creek, his ocean of imagination.

He wiped at his eyes, and started toward the foot bridge. Mrs. Clancy had told him to take some time for himself, and he was going to take her up on that. After he'd dropped Tom off at home, he'd driven around the town in which he'd grown up. It had changed so much.

There were three new housing developments, which meant thousands of new residents. There was a new middle school, and talk of a new high school to accommodate all the new families. There was a Walmart now, and it seemed to thrive in comparison to the K-Mart he'd frequented as a kid. Driving down the main street, which was longer now with more lanes, there were as many chain restaurants and businesses as there were local ones. The small town he'd grown up in wasn't so small anymore. Luckily, however, it still had the small feel. Though, that might have just been his perception. Anything looked small and uncrowded in comparison to Manhattan.

His pace across the bridge and down the walking path slowed. Rubbing his hand over his cheeks, he felt the fall evening air moving in and it chilled him. Or perhaps, knowing his sister died there, chilled him more.

Shadows darkened the path. Branches hovered above him, some with lingering leaves, others bare.

"Taking a stroll, Matthews?" Lacy's voice cut through the quiet.

He turned to see her walking toward him, her hands in the pockets of her black jacket.

"Trying to clear my head."

"And this is where you chose?" she asked as she came to stand next to him.

"I have more good memories here than bad ones."

A smile formed on her lips, though it didn't match her eyes, which were dark and tired. "I assume when you grew up here, there weren't as many people on this path running."

He shook his head. "Lot more trees, less traffic. It was secluded."

Reaching her hand out to him, she touched his arm. "I remember."

Declan slid a glance to her hand. "What a time, huh?"

She moved her hand down until it gripped his. "You might not believe it, but I think of it fondly. It was hard to settle in here, to move on from what happened to my family. You helped me settle, Matthews."

He felt that unraveling feeling move over him again, with her hand holding his. Perhaps that's what caused him to pull her to him, embracing her tightly as he warded off the rush of pain that attacked him.

LACY'S FIRST THOUGHT WAS TO PUSH BACK, BUT SHE'D instigated this, she decided, by opening up. That's why she didn't do it very often. However, it seemed to have brought him comfort —exposing her pain. What did it hurt to let him hold her?

Pressing her palms to his back, she rested her head on his chest. That broad chest, she remembered, and her stomach tightened. How many times had she thought of resting her head right there? Too many. And it had always seemed so silly to her to think of him. He'd been her first. That alone was why she figured she'd thought so much of him. But then again, she'd known it was more than that. He'd been her first love too, but she was sure he didn't know that part. How could he? After a few weeks, and a few times together, she'd given him the cold shoulder. She'd pushed him right out of her life.

The fact that he was giving her this moment was special. And it wasn't for her at all, she reminded herself as his hands moved compassionately over her back. This was her offering to him. Her comfort for his loss. Her loss was so long ago, and no one offered this kind of compassion back then.

He eased back, only slightly. Lifting his palm to her cheek, he held it there, and she saw the tears that welled in his eyes.

"How did you handle this as a child? I hurt so bad it's hard to breathe, but I have to be strong for everyone else."

"There are a lot of people around, Matthews. Why do you have to be so strong?"

His thumb brushed her cheekbone. "I've always been the strong one." He sniffed and batted his eyes dry. "Her kids..."

"Will survive. But they will need all of you. Trust me on that."

"You're so strong."

"I broke many times," she confessed as his hand lingered so

gently on her face. "I've hit rock bottom a thousand times. I watched my father crash too. You're never going to forget."

"I don't think I want to. But, damn, I couldn't imagine it would hurt this bad."

"I hate to break it to you, you haven't felt bad yet."

He pulled her to him again, and as before, she let him just hold her. They stood there in the dimming light, the fall air cooling, until they heard the sound of someone running on the path beyond the trees.

Quickly, they stepped back from one another, just as Pastor Ralph jogged around the corner.

He panted and slowed as he saw them. Checking his fitness band, he stopped with his hands on his hips. "Lacy. Declan. Are you both out for a run?" he asked.

Declan shoved his hands in his pockets. "Just clearing my mind. Lacy was kind enough to let me bend her ear."

Pastor Ralph smiled. "You're going through a hard time, Declan. My door is open to you any time."

"I appreciate that."

"Lacy is a good listener too. She has her mother's compassion."

The comparison slashed at Lacy. Hadn't she learned so many years after her mother's death that lending an ear had been the pathway to her mother's infidelity? She'd befriended a married man, been his innocent confidant, and then an extramarital relationship followed.

Lacy swallowed hard. Declan wasn't married, so she shouldn't take the pastor's words as anything but complimentary. In fact, she didn't even quite believe them. Lacy had never been someone's comfort in that way. That's what made her a good detective. Even in knowing the victim, she didn't get emotionally sidetracked.

Pastor Ralph checked his wrist monitor again. "Again, Declan, if I can do anything more for you or your family, please call."

"I will."

"I'll see you both on Friday." He gave them a polite nod and jogged away.

When he was out of sight, Declan let out a long breath. "I feel guilty when that man is around."

"Guilty of what?"

He chuckled. "Anything. Everything."

Lacy nodded in agreement. "He has a way."

"I didn't realize he knew your mother."

"Clergy move around every few years. Pastor Ralph was some of the reason my dad decided to settle here. It was far enough away from our tragedy, and yet this was where Pastor Ralph had relocated. He'd counseled my dad so he was comforted in knowing that he had someone."

"Counseled him after your mom died?"

Lacy folded her hands in front of her, rubbing her palm with her thumb as she would do to keep herself calm. "And before. My parents had stumbled upon a rocky time before she died. It's all old news. It was enough to have the authorities suspect my father for a while, but his alibi was solid. He was with me at a school function when my mother was killed."

Declan reached for her hand, but she flinched and pulled back. He then tucked his hands back into his pockets. "I'm so sorry, Lacy. I don't even know how you do the work you do every day. It has to bring up so many horrible memories."

"Like I said, if I can someday keep another child from going through what I did, then it's all been worth it."

Declan looked out over the wooded area where they'd found Stacy the morning before. His shoulders dropped, and he swayed back on his heels. "I suppose I should get going. My parents are probably tired of being babysat by the neighbor."

"I'll walk back to the lot with you," she said as if it were an offer to him, but she wanted a few more minutes to simply have him near her.

They walked silently back to the lot. "I'll be in touch, Matthews. I'm going to find that asshole that did this."

"I know you will," he said as he pulled open the car door. "In fact, I'm banking on it."

He waited until she slid into her car and shut the door before he climbed into his car. Then he waited for her to back out of the lot before he did the same.

She'd been shot at, punched in the face, and verbally assaulted numerous times over the past ten years. She could certainly hold her own against anyone, but she found it comforting that a man would make sure she was safely on her way before he drove away.

As she hit the street and turned left, she watched in her review mirror as he turned right. Gripping the steering wheel a bit tighter, she cursed herself for having followed him to the trail. Though she'd fantasized about holding him as she had, she hadn't expected it. It was stupid to keep thinking about it.

Declan Matthews was desperate for companionship and comfort. If she gave it to him, she'd be the one who was destined for heartbreak. The man left fifteen years ago and hardly returned. And when he did, he'd kept to himself and close to family. Once this was all over, there was no reason to think he'd stick around too long. He had a life thousands of miles away from his childhood home.

For the moment, Lacy was part of his life, though assigned to be and not originally by choice. He'd forget all about her when he was back in his Manhattan office.

Turning toward the McDonald's, she let out a low growl. She was only hurting herself thinking that the hug on the trail meant a thing, but it did to her. Declan would always be on her mind, that was just the way it was. So, as she would any other time, she pulled into the drive-thru and ordered french fries. After she paid and received her order, she headed to the rec center. A nice long swim, followed by leg day would get her mind off Declan, and it would afford her the fries she was about to drown her sorrows in.

❧ 10 ❧

Sobs heard through the walls had kept Declan up most the night. He heard his father get up a number of times, and his mother's crying was almost unbearable.

He'd risen and met his father in the hallway or the kitchen three times during the night. After having to have had his mother hospitalized the night his sister died, he didn't want to have to do that again.

"She'll be okay," his father assured him as he carried a glass of warm milk toward his bedroom. "She keeps having nightmares about how Stacy's going to look during visitation. I know she'll look beautiful. I think that'll give her some peace."

Declan nodded, and then scrubbed his hands over his tired face. "Dad, she didn't look bad when I saw her. Let Mom know that. Let her know that she was peaceful."

"She's gone, Dec. I don't think even that will help, but I'll tell her."

Declan's father gave him a pat on the back and then continued on to his bedroom.

Declan stood in the hallway for a moment and listened to his mother's inconsolable cries. He rolled his head in a circular motion to release the tension in his neck.

Walking back to his room, he shut the door. It was nearly three in the morning, and he wondered if he was ever going to get back to sleep.

Crawling into bed, he picked up his phone and scrolled through his emails. There were many condolences from co-workers and clients. Friends he hadn't seen since he left town were reaching out to him. Even his bitch of an ex-wife had emailed. How could the woman who wanted to rip him off write such an eloquent email giving her sympathies to his family? He wanted to be mad—he was mad. But the anger fizzled. He couldn't even direct it toward her. The problem was, he didn't know where his anger was supposed to be aimed. He didn't have a name or a face to the person who caused him such pain.

He could only assume that was Lacy's problem too. He'd seen that beautiful face turn to anger and hate in a moment. Now he understood it better. And he didn't like that they could now connect on this level.

Tomorrow they'd lay his sister to rest, and none of them would ever be at peace again, he thought, as he turned his phone off completely with the hope of getting a few hours of sleep.

⚜

Lacy listened to the anonymous message again and wrote down the details.

The leads they had on Stacy's case were few: Stacy stopped in to the Starbucks, where she'd worked, at four o'clock and had gotten a cup of coffee—a grande caramel macchiato. One witness said he'd seen her sitting in her car at four-fifteen in the lot by the trail, when he'd slipped on his running shoes and headed out for his afternoon run. She'd given him a wave. They didn't know each other, just that they frequented the same path. He said he'd usually run for an hour, but on that afternoon he'd only run ten minutes when the soccer coach had called to tell him that his daughter had twisted her ankle. At that time he'd run back toward the parking lot. The message went on to say he saw Stacy back in the trees, specifically on the fallen tree, and she was with a man. He had on a black sweatshirt with the hood up, and white running shoes. He had an arm draped over her shoulders, and the man would guess that she was crying.

He went on to say, he didn't think anything about it. They looked comfortable as if they were friends. He was too worried about getting to the school.

Lacy tapped her pen to her chin. So if she usually met Vaughn in the afternoon, why was she there if he had a meeting and her husband was home? And how was it that she was what she considered a good friend with Stacy, yet she had no idea she was having an affair with Vaughn, and perhaps this other man.

What was wrong with the world when seemingly happy women took up with other men, especially when they had children. It just didn't make sense to her.

She made a note of the witness' phone number, and looked up his address in the system. Before she met up with him, she'd check his alibi, and then question him.

⚜

DECLAN OPENED THE FRONT DOOR TO HIS PARENTS' HOUSE when the doorbell rang for the twelfth time in an hour. This time Vaughn stood on the other side, a bouquet of flowers in one hand and a grocery bag in the other.

"I wanted to drop this by. I plan to go to the viewing tonight, but I'm on call, and…"

"Thanks," Declan said as he stepped back to let Vaughn through. "My mom is in the kitchen. I'll take you back and you can give her the flowers."

"I brought some food too. I don't know why, but it seemed like the right thing to do."

"She'll appreciate it."

His mother was standing at the back door staring out into the back yard, a cup of coffee resting between her hands. She looked pale, Declan thought as he moved toward her, and she didn't seem to notice them walk in.

"Mom," he said gently and she raised her eyes to his. "Vaughn stopped by." He motioned to his friend who stood at the kitchen island holding the items he'd brought.

His mother blinked a few times, as if to bring herself back to the moment. "Vaughn, it's nice to see you. Thank you for helping Declan out this week. Seems I had a little episode the other night, and..."

"Mrs. Matthews, it was my pleasure. Anything I can do to ease your pain at this time, please let me know."

"I appreciate that, Vaughn."

"I brought these for you," he nodded to the bouquet. "And some groceries too. Just some sandwich fixings. It's not much, but..."

"It's a wonderful gesture." She turned back to Declan. "Would you see to all that. I'm going to go up and make sure your father is okay. He was resting. I kept him up the better part of the night," she offered, handing Declan her cup and then walking out of the kitchen.

Declan sipped the coffee, and swallowed hard when he realized it was stone cold. "I don't know how long she was nursing this," he said as he moved to the sink and dumped it out.

"She doesn't look good," Vaughn whispered.

"She was up all night crying. She had Dad and I both up. They gave her some sleeping pills at the hospital, but she won't use them."

"She might when everything settles. It's a lot to absorb."

Declan rested his hip against the counter. "What's Lacy's story? I mean is she all work? Is she seeing anyone?"

The expression on Vaughn's face shifted to humored, and perhaps a tad bit horrified. "That's what you're thinking about right now?"

Declan shrugged. "It's something to occupy my head. Something other than what's surrounding me."

Vaughn gave him a slow thoughtful nod as he leaned against the island and crossed his arms in front of him.

"To tell you the truth, I don't know. I see Lacy maybe once a month around town." He winced as he looked down at the floor. "More when there's a case like Stacy's or Carley's."

"Did they question you about Carley's death? Since you two..."

Vaughn winced. "Yes. I was out of town. Out of the state even."

"They were both killed," he swallowed hard when he said the word, "in the same area. It says serial killer to me." Declan let out a long breath to steady himself after saying the words aloud.

"Did Lacy tell you that?"

He shook his head. "No. She hasn't said much about it. Just filled me in on whatever they know, which is nothing."

Vaughn rubbed his chin, and then his palms together. "I should let you get to your parents. I plan on stopping by the viewing, if that's okay with you."

"Of course," Declan said as he watched the nervous energy consume his friend. "I appreciate all you've done for us."

"Wish there was more I could do. I'll see you later."

Declan watched Vaughn hurry out of the kitchen, and a moment later the front door closed.

❧ 11 ❧

L acy parked in the space furthest from the door of the funeral home. She hated viewings. She hated it more when the person laying in wake was a friend.

It still stung knowing that Vaughn and Stacy had been having an affair. She wasn't sure if it was because she hadn't known, because it was with Vaughn, or because it was something that dredged up horrible thoughts in her head.

When she thought of a woman having an affair, it always took her back to the moment she'd found out about her mother's affair. It had made her feel dirty and less worthy, and it had had nothing to do with her at all. At least that's what she always convinced herself of after years of therapy. Her mother was in an unhappy state in her life when she chose to spend time with a man that wasn't her husband. Lacy couldn't carry the guilt of it for the rest of her life.

She'd gone through all the stages of mourning over, and over again. Now, after all these years, she wasn't angry at her mother anymore. And being angry with someone that was ripped from your life was a horrible thing to be.

Lacy looked toward the door as Declan walked outside. He

was dressed in a gray suit. Shielding his eyes with a dark pair of sunglasses, he moved into fading sunshine and lifted his face to it.

She wondered how long it would take before he cracked. Would he? Would he fall apart when it was all over? Or was he the kind of man he appeared to be? Strong and solid—unshakable.

As he lowered his face, he scanned the parking lot, and that must have been when he noticed her parked in the lot. She could have sworn a smile formed on his lips, and he started toward her car.

Lacy opened her car door and stepped out.

"Whoa, Pratt! You're wearing a dress." He was grinning as he said it.

"It's a skirt. For someone who's as sharply dressed as you, I'd think you'd know the difference."

"Yeah, I do. Casual skirt, flats, a light jacket," he said as he brushed his hand down her arm. "You look sharp, too."

She had to swallow hard before she spoke. "Declan, I'm so sorry about Stacy. I'm broken-hearted for her and her family. And for you."

"You've said that." He pulled the dark glasses from his face and she saw the red rimmed eyes of a man who was in mourning. "It looks like you're off duty tonight."

"Unless a big lead comes in."

"Have dinner with me. I need that non-family contact now, not after this is all done." He lifted his chin. "Unless that crosses some line."

"If a call comes in, I have to go. But, Dec, we were friends first, before I was in law enforcement. I don't have to worry about crossing a line if you're my friend."

He reached for her hand and pulled her to him. Her cheek pressed against his chest as his arms came around her and held her there. "I need a friend right now, that's for sure."

"I'm here," she said before she realized she had.

Lacy stood still, and when he had taken all he could from the embrace, he pulled back and looked down and into her eyes. "She looks beautiful. The kids came earlier and their grandmother took them home before people arrived."

"How did they do?"

He reached up and brushed a strand of hair from her face, tucking it behind her ear as if it were the normal thing for him to do to her. "Andi kept telling her to wake up. She wanted to lay with her," he said as a tear streaked down his cheek and he quickly brushed it away. "Toby stood on the other side of the room. He didn't want to see her."

She could feel the tears building in her throat. She remembered being just like Toby. She'd only seen her mother from afar when they'd had her viewing. Most of the time she'd hidden in the bathroom. But before they closed her casket, when the mourners had left, Lacy had asked for a few moments alone.

It had been the first time she'd seen anyone that was dead. Having it be her mother brought her no comfort. It had been before she'd learned of her infidelity, which Lacy took personally. It had been an innocent time where a little girl lost her mother.

She'd written her a letter, and she took a moment to read it to her, standing there alone, then she'd slipped it under her mother's cold hands. She would never forget her cold hands, because her mother was never cold.

"I remember not wanting to see my mother too," she said. "They're getting the kids help, right?"

"Yeah. And we're going to make sure they're okay."

"Declan!" They both turned when they heard Vaughn call for him.

"That's my sign that my mother is looking for me." He released her and she suddenly felt the chill in the air. "I'll walk in with you."

They walked in silence toward the door. Vaughn gave them a smile, his lips tightly pressed together.

Lacy stopped as Declan opened the door. "Go on in. I'll be just a moment."

Declan gave her a nod and walked inside.

Lacy leaned against the pillar next to where Vaughn stood. "How are you holding up?"

"This isn't about me, Lace."

"Question stands. I'm being human, Vaughn. Not a cop."

He chewed on his bottom lip a moment. "She looks beautiful. Just like she did the last time I saw her."

She'd seen murderers at funerals and how they reacted to the deceased. Vaughn was shaken. It was visible in how he looked, stood, breathed. His alibis were solid, and looking at him, she'd say he was innocent. But not until she had a killer in custody would she let him completely off the hook.

"Are you sticking around a bit longer?"

"Actually I'm heading out. I just got a call from work. I'm on call tonight, so it looks like they can't handle it without me. I'm headed to the office."

"I understand that. I'm on call too." She rested her hand on his arm. "Take care of yourself, Vaughn," she said as she walked past him and into the funeral home.

There was a smell to funeral homes that she never could quite stomach. Potpourri, flowers, and an eerie clean scent that made her feel as if they tried too hard to cover the stench of death. Then again, she thought as she looked around at people talking in quiet groups, most of them didn't know that stench like she did. They hadn't seen bodies mutilated and dumped in places people were never meant to find them.

Resting her hand on her stomach, she walked toward the casket where her friend lay now dressed up as if she were going to the theater for the night. Tucked all around her were drawings that no doubt Andi had colored for her mother. She hated the saying *they look peaceful,* but Stacy did.

She reached her hand out and touched Stacy's arm. That zap of cold had her nearly pulling her hand back, but she refrained.

"I'll miss you," she said in a whisper and then gasped as someone brushed up next to her.

"Doesn't she look peaceful?" Pastor Ralph Burton asked, looking down at Stacy. "Such a shame."

"She looks beautiful."

"Any new leads?" he asked.

She looked at Stacy and then at Pastor Ralph. It seemed like an inappropriate conversation to have over the casket of a murder victim. "We're following up on everything that might lead to one."

He patted her cheek with his hand, as he would when she was younger. "I know you'll do right by her," he said before moving toward another parishioner from his church.

"I will do right by you," she said to Stacy as Declan moved in next to her.

"My mother picked out the dress."

"It looks nice on her," Lacy said. "Where is your mother? I want to pay my respects."

He turned and nodded to the corner where there was a couch. His mother sat there, Mrs. Clancy at her side, and a circle of women whom Lacy knew as Mrs. Matthews' book club stood talking with her.

As she turned from the casket, Declan by her side, Mr. Matthews walked toward them.

"Mr. Matthews, I'm so sorry for your loss."

"Thank you," he sighed. "This is nothing a parent ever wants to go through."

"I know."

"Find them, Lacy." Mr. Matthews looked her right in the eye, and the heat from the words seared right into her heart. "Make them pay for this. They took my daughter away. They took a mother from her children." His voice began to shake and Declan moved toward him, putting an arm around his shoulders.

"Dad, she's going to do everything she can," he urged. "Lacy's good at what she does."

"Yes, sir. I'll find the person responsible."

Mr. Matthews took in a few deep breaths and moved toward Pastor Ralph who summoned him.

"He's unsteady," Declan offered.

"He's hurt, angry, sad. I get it. I'm going to talk to your mother and then head out. I'll admit, I'm not usually too welcome at these things. People think I haven't done my job if we get this far and no one has been caught."

"I have no doubt you're doing everything in your power."

She knew it was supposed to be a compliment, or agreement to the fact that she'd find the bastard responsible, but his tone had hitched when he'd said it.

"I am." She turned from him and walked toward his mother. The air was getting thick in the room, and she was going to need to make her exit as quickly as possible.

She would find the bastard and bring them to their knees. It might have been fifteen years since she'd been around Declan, but she never wanted to see that hint of disdain in his eyes again.

12

Lacy walked from the funeral home, with a fire in her belly. She was going to blow off Declan's dinner invite, hit the gym at the station, and order a pizza while she sat at her desk and pored over the evidence they did have—which wasn't much. Something had to be missing. This was too close for comfort, and too much like Carley Francess-Hastings' murder to be coincidence. Someone had a grievance against these two women, and the only bond they had was Vaughn Price.

It was pissing her off that he had solid alibis, because that would give her some kind of break in this case. Then she thought of his eyes, and how he acted. He didn't seem guilty, and that pissed her off too. She liked Vaughn just fine, but she'd like to know the killer of two women was behind bars.

"Lacy."

She turned as she heard her name and saw Pastor Ralph walk toward her. "Thank you for coming. It means a lot to the family. I know you were Stacy's friend. If you need to talk about this, I'm here for you too, dear."

"I appreciate that."

He took her hand in his and patted it. "How is your father?"

"He's fine." She wished she had a better word. "He's on vacation in Alaska right now. One of those big fishing trips. Month away with some guys." She forced the smile to her face.

"What a wonderful adventure."

She nodded. "I didn't see your wife here."

He pursed his lips. "She's been sick the past few weeks. Hasn't gotten out of bed much. Some bug just holding on." He smiled, still gripping her hand. "She'll be happy to know you asked about her."

Again, just as he had before, he patted her cheek and turned to talk to others leaving the funeral home.

Lacy started toward her car in the far corner of the lot, and slowed her stride when she noticed that Vaughn's car was parked only a few spaces from hers. Not the time to be unarmed and in a skirt, she thought. A few moments later she noticed he was walking toward his car from the other side of the lot. A quick take, and she noticed Autumn Taylor walking toward the funeral home.

Lacy clenched her fists to her side. Vaughn was a pig. There were a hundred people milling around that parking lot and he's talking to a married woman, whom she knew he'd had an affair with. It made her sick. And hadn't she told him to lay low for a bit?

God, what was it with men not being able to control themselves?

"Lacy."

She spun at the sound of her name again. "What?" She snapped as she noticed Declan stop his quickened step toward her. Guilt pierced through her chest. "I'm sorry. I had my head wrapped around something. I didn't mean to... oh, hell. Sorry."

"You don't seem like the kind of woman who says sorry much, so I'll take it. I'm going to be about an hour here. Tom is taking my parents home. He's looking for an excuse to not go home right away."

"He needs time to clear his head."

"Yeah. Anyway, I'll pick you up, say six-thirty?"

Lacy winced. "Why don't you head home? You've had a long day and..."

"And you're shooting me down." His voice dipped with the disappointment.

"I just think I should get back to the station, do some work, try to find this maniac that's terrorizing everyone."

"When will you find time to eat? Can't keep your strength up if you don't eat."

Lacy coughed out a laugh. Declan didn't remember her much at all. She ate plenty, and worked it off plenty too. "I'll order up a pizza."

"You shouldn't eat at your desk."

"Lawyers never eat at their desks?"

He took a breath to speak, then let it drain. "I'll see you at the funeral tomorrow."

She nodded as he turned to walk way, and she continued toward her car, and just in time to see Vaughn pull away from the parking space and head out onto the road.

If she hurried, she could follow him for a bit, just to see where he actually ended up.

VAUGHN HAD DRIVEN AWAY FROM THE FUNERAL HOME AND straight to the liquor store. Lacy watched him walk out with a six pack of Bud Light and a bottle of wine, which he tucked up under his arm as he opened the car door. After a few minutes, and a phone call, he left the parking lot and she followed him right to his office. Taking the badge from his pocket, he clipped it to his jacket, and walked through the door. Once inside the building, he stopped and talked to the security guard at the desk, and then disappeared into an elevator.

Lacy sat parked across the street. Another ten minutes, she

thought as she turned down the radio, as if it helped her concentrate on the front door of the building and the people that walked in front of it.

When Vaughn didn't reemerge quickly, she decided to go with her original plan, and headed back to the station.

Lacy parked in her normal parking space at the back of the lot. There weren't a lot of people there past six anyway, but she wanted those extra steps to count on the fitness monitor. Besides, she was eating the whole pizza she was going to order, and drinking the two-liter of Coke she was getting too.

She pulled her gym bag from the backseat, and headed toward the front door. Just as she approached the door, and it slid open, she saw Declan standing there, leaned up against the front desk talking to Alberta, who floated the front desk when she wasn't working dispatch.

Her keen senses should have smelled the pizza he was holding long before she'd ever noticed him standing there with it, but it hadn't been until he stood erect, that she'd seen it.

"What are you doing here, Matthews?"

"I still think you have to eat. I was thinking something a little better than pizza, but you said it was on the menu for tonight. I also brought some bottles of cold sparkling water, plates and napkins, and if you're good and eat all your dinner, there's brownies too."

It took everything she had in her to scowl at him and grunt as if she was going to kick him in the shins, because the truth was, her mouth was watering.

"And if I don't?"

He chuckled. "I told Alberta I was going to save her a brownie anyway, but I'll give them all to her now."

She looked at the woman, who actually looked as if she'd harm Lacy just to get those brownies. Lacy wasn't one to go down in a challenge. Alberta could have her one brownie, but Lacy was getting her share.

"Fine, Matthews, but this could be considered stalking," she informed him as she walked toward the elevator and pushed the button.

"Or it's the lawyer looking for information for his client. You know, wrongful doings and all."

She spun to look him in the eye. "What, are you going to sue us or something?"

He actually took a step back. "I was just going along with your misguided rant, Lace. Chill out."

She turned back to the shiny metal door, and she could see him keeping a close eye on her. She hated when someone called her out on a mood, and that's exactly what he'd just done.

"You as quick on your feet as you are with your witty comebacks, Slick?" She turned, took the bag of drinks and plates from him.

"You running out the front door?"

She chuckled. "Elevators are slow. I never take them. I was being easy on you. But you look like you could maneuver three flights of stairs with a box of pizza in your hand."

"Lead the way."

DECLAN HADN'T EXPECTED ANY LESS THAN THE SASS THAT LACY was dishing out to him. He'd been short with her at the funeral home, and that hadn't sat well with him. Hence his showing up with pizza after she shot him down for dinner.

She pushed through the door to the stairwell, and began taking them two steps at a time. He was sure that was to show him up, and it did. He worked on the twenty-eighth floor, and lived on the tenth. Taking the stairs wasn't something he opted for very often. Lacy had him there.

When he reached the third floor, she stood waiting for him holding open the door.

"Thought you'd never get here," she joked, straight faced.

"I just don't think you wanted me looking at your ass the whole time."

Her mouth opened and shut again quickly. "Watch it, Matthews."

"I thought we were going to work on that first name thing again," he reminded her as he followed her to her desk.

"When I think you deserve it. Right now, I'm not there."

She pulled out her chair and sat down. Declan looked around the less-than-tidy work space, set the pizza on the desk, and took one of the chairs that faced her desk.

"I'm guessing all of this is organized."

She nodded and flipped open the top of the pizza box. "I know where everything on this desk is. Don't mess with anything."

"I get it. You should see me when I'm going over a case."

"I don't want to think about it. If you're a neat and tidy guy, great. At least I know, with some confidence, that I could go to the bathroom at your house and not have to clean the toilet first."

The laugh broke through as he reached for a plate and a slice of pizza. "I'd like to think that was the case. Besides, I'm optimistic. You're thinking about my place as a place you might want to go someday."

She lifted her eyes and they'd gone wide. "Declan, I was just..."

"I know." He sat down in the chair and took a bite of his pizza. "I'm hurt because you canceled on me. You're in a mood because I put you in one. Like I said before, I just want to be around someone who isn't family for a bit. So, if I have to sit here and eat this amazing pizza, by the way, by myself, I'll do it."

"Gino's Pizza is the best in town. I would have ordered from there if I had made it that far."

"What would you have ordered?" he asked taking another bite.

"Pepperoni, just like you did."

"I knew it." Declan pulled a bottle of water from the bag and handed it to her, then took one for himself and opened it. "You know there's a place down the street from my condo called Gino's. I'll stop in when I'm missing home. It's not the same at all, but it does the job when I'm homesick."

Lacy leaned back in her seat and kicked her feet up on her desk. "Where do you live exactly?"

Declan took a long, thoughtful sip of his water. "Central Park West." She shrugged and took a bite of her pizza. Usually telling someone he lived on Central Park West raised a brow. "Never been to New York?"

"Buffalo. Does that count?"

"Not in this case." He bit into his pizza and watched her. "When I wake up every morning I look out over Central Park."

"Central Park is really big, right? Is that a big deal?"

She was taking all his glory away as she sat there eating pizza and looking unimpressed.

"To some."

"So you're a good lawyer? I mean if you can live in a condo that overlooks Central Park."

Now she was getting it. "Yeah, I'd like to think I'm a good lawyer."

"Well, detectives don't live in nice condos, wear fancy suits, and have designer sunglasses."

"Didn't realize we were trying to one up each other."

Lacy lowered her feet to the ground. "We're not. I'm in a mood, and I'm sorry."

"Again with the sorry. You must think a lot of me to worry about my feelings so much."

She laughed now and eased back in her chair, balancing her plate on her lap. "It's a dark time."

"That it is."

THEY'D EATEN THE ENTIRE PIZZA. LACY HAD DRUNK THE WATER

he brought, but she was dying for a Coke. She'd stop on her way home and get one. But one thing was for sure, with him sitting across from her, she wasn't going to get any work done. Besides, he'd lightened her mood, and now she was gazing at him. She needed to go home.

"I'm not going to get anything done. I think I'll head home," she said as she tossed her paper plate and napkin into the empty box.

"Yeah, me too. Tomorrow's going to be a long day."

"I'm going to try to be there, and I will be if nothing comes up."

He smiled with one side of his mouth. "We'd appreciate that."

Declan stood and picked up the box. "Trash can?"

"There's one in the break room by the stairs."

"You're going to make me walk down the stairs after we ate a whole pizza?"

"Now you have to, or you'll get a tire around your middle," she joked.

"You never eat this much pizza do you?" he asked following her to the break room.

"You have no idea."

She turned on the light in the room, took the box, and discarded it. After a moment of thought, she went to the refrigerator and took out a Coke, clearly marked for her partner. She'd get it replaced by the morning.

Lacy turned off the lights and started back for the stairs. When they'd passed off the last brownie to Alberta, which Lacy had made sure was ample enough, they headed out to the parking lot.

"Where are you parked?" Declan asked.

"I always park in the south forty," she said with a laugh. "Gotta work off pizza and this soda."

"I'll walk you to your car."

"I'm the one with the gun and the training. I'll be fine."

"I'll walk you anyway."

And he did walk her silently all the way to the car. "Thanks for the pizza," she offered as she pulled open her car door. "Want a ride back to your car?"

"I'll be fine."

He stood there for a moment, not moving away as she'd expected him to do. And she stood there, looking up into those eyes that sparkled in the dark. "Well, goodnight."

That's when he pulled her in and took her mouth with his. The urgent need, and the warmth of it took her under fast and she wrapped her arms around his neck to hold on tight. His tongue flicked against hers and the heat of the moment had her gasping for breath.

She wanted to say something—anything, but there were no words as his hand moved up her back and into her hair. Lust and need swirled in her belly and contradicted the stern talking to she was giving herself. She wanted this. Oh, God, how she wanted this.

"Is there anything in this whole world I could do to persuade you to keep doing this?" he asked as his lips moved from hers and traveled down her throat and to her collar bone.

Her chest heaved against his. Her brain said no, it screamed it. Now wasn't the time to get involved with the brother of a victim —even if it was Declan. But, oh, her heart fought the very vivid argument going on in her head.

"Follow me to my..." she began just as her phone rang with the very distinct tone that said her evening had just been interrupted by a crime.

Her hands came up between them, encouraging Declan to take a step back. Lacy pulled the phone from her pocket and lifted it to her ear. "Moss, what have we got?"

She listened and when she pressed her hand to her forehead, Declan moved in closer, touching her back. "I'll be there in ten," she informed him, and then disconnected the call.

Lacy jerked from Declan's. touch, throwing her phone into the passenger seat. "I have to go," she said quickly as she climbed into the car, but he stood between her and the door. "Move, Matthews."

"Oh, we're back to that."

"Hey, job calls."

"What's up? What happened?"

"Job. Move."

"I saw the look on your face. Tell me where you're going."

Lacy put the keys in the ignition and started the car. "They just found the body of Autumn Taylor a half mile from where your sister was found."

He gripped the door. "I just talked to Autumn two hours ago."

"Yeah, well someone must not have liked that too much." She reached for the door. "Go home, Declan."

He backed up, and she watched him in the review mirror, standing there as she sped away to the murder scene of another person she knew personally.

13

Moss ran toward her the moment Lacy stepped out of the car.

"Twenty goddamned minutes!" He yelled as he approached. "Her body is still warm." He raked his fingers through his hair.

"Who found her? Who called it in?"

"Some old lady walking her dog. Lives across the creek where those patio homes back up to the path. Dog went out to poop, got spooked, and ran into the wooded area. She followed."

"She didn't see anything?"

"All she saw was a figure running out of the area, on foot, no car. She thought it was a jogger. She's pretty shaken up. They called in her son to come get her. Paramedics are giving her oxygen. She's in a robe for God's sake."

"We need a location on Vaughn Price, now." She pulled her phone out of her pocket.

"You think he has something to do with this?"

They began walking the now much too familiar path back to the wooded area to where another body waited for them.

"Around five o'clock, when I left the funeral home Vaughn was in the parking lot talking to Autumn. So I thought I'd follow him. He'd told me he was on call for work and they'd just called him in."

"He didn't go to work?"

"Stopped at the liquor store first. Bought a six pack of Bud Light and a bottle of wine. Walked back to his car, made a phone call, and then I followed him to his office building. Waited outside for ten minutes to see if he came back out, but he didn't, so I left."

"We'll bring him in for questioning and check the security footage of the building."

Lacy stopped walking and turned to Carl. "I'll bring him in. If he's lying to us, I'm going to take him down myself. I'm not going to have a killer look me in the eye and turn around and kill again."

"If it is Vaughn, he's not going anywhere. He wants to be seen so no one thinks a thing about it."

"You're right. But we can take him in on suspicion."

Carl nodded in agreement and they continued their walk toward the body of Autumn Taylor.

Just like the other two victims, Autumn was fully clothed, and might have been mistaken for someone sleeping, if someone walked past her.

"She's been strangled, but no fingerprints." The medical examiner looked up at Lacy as she stood over the body. "There are shoe prints around here, but I'm not sure they'll do us any good. This is a makeout point for the kids."

Carl nodded. "Turk said he's busted five couples in this area in the last four days."

"Crap. Okay. I'm heading over to Vaughn's and bringing him in." She turned and Carl grabbed her arm.

"*You're* doing that? On your own? You're going to go face a potential murderer on your own? What's gotten into you?"

"Vaughn isn't dangerous to me."

"And don't you think that's what she thought, too?" he asked pointing to Autumn's body. "These women knew their killer. Not one of them struggled against him. If it is Vaughn, and I think it is, then we go together. We have back up. There's none of this crap about you going alone."

She hated being scolded by someone she had seniority over, but he was right. And she knew what had gotten into her head. That kiss Declan had put on her messed up her head. But she was focused now. Vaughn was going to pay for what he'd done.

LACY HAD BARELY PUT THE CAR IN PARK WHEN SHE RIPPED HER seat belt off and pushed from the car. Carl was right behind her, and three more squad cars created a barrier for them. One on each end of the street, another two doors down, and she had word one was out back.

Lacy pulled on her vest and fixed the holster. She still wore the stupid skirt she'd had on when she went to the viewing. Internally, she vowed to never get caught like that again. "We don't need all this crap," she said as she finalized her equipment.

"He's killing, Lace. He'll kill you, too."

No. No, she'd kill him. She was quite sure of it.

Lacy started for the door, Carl right behind her, and the other officers poised with guns drawn. She had her hand on her weapon as she rang the doorbell.

"Hold on. I'm coming." Vaughn's voice nearly sang from behind the door. "I was waiting for you," he said as pulled open the door and she pulled her gun. She wasn't going to let him take her by surprise.

But it was Vaughn that looked surprised when he saw her standing there, Carl behind her, his gun drawn, and the cars in the street.

Vaughn stood there with a glass of wine now in each hand, and an apron with the body of a woman in a bikini on over the clothes she'd seen him wear to the viewing.

His eyes were wide, and she could see his hands begin to shake. A moment later one of the glasses slipped from his hand and crashed to the floor.

Lacy eased toward the door and Vaughn didn't move.

"Relax," she said carefully holstering her gun as Carl moved in behind her. "We need to talk."

Vaughn blinked hard and then focused back on her. "Lacy, what's going on? What are you doing? They have guns. Why do they have guns?"

"We're here to take you in."

His breath came harder now. "Me in where?"

"We need to take you down to the station and ask you some questions."

"Okay." She noticed the sweat forming on his forehead. "You've asked me questions. What's this about?"

"Who was the other glass of wine for, Vaughn?"

"What?" He looked down at the mess on the floor. "Oh. Yeah. I'm waiting for Autumn."

Lacy exchanged a glance with Carl, then focused back on Vaughn. "Autumn is coming here?"

"Yes. God, did her husband find out? I'm so sorry." Tears filled his eyes and then spilled over and down his cheeks. "I didn't want to hurt anyone. She just wanted to talk."

Lacy eased toward Vaughn and took the glass from his shanking hand, and set it on the floor. "When did you talk to her?"

He raked his hands through his hair. "At the funeral home. It was quick. She caught me in the parking lot and asked if she could come over and talk. I told her to be here at nine. Then I went to the liquor store. She called me when I got back to the car and said she'd left the funeral home and was going home. She was going to tell her husband that she was going out with the girls. I went to my office after that. I was there an hour." He frowned down at the floor. "Yeah, about an hour. They had a server problem and I got them back up and running. Then I came home and made a nice dinner." He lifted his eyes to Lacy. "Autumn is on her way."

"Do you have dinner cooking right now?"

"Yeah. It's supposed to come out of the oven in a minute."

"Why don't we go in and you can take that out. Can I sit and talk to you for a minute?"

"Something's wrong, Lace. God, what's wrong."

"C'mon, let's go to the kitchen."

Lacy rested a hand on Vaughn's shoulder and they walked slowly to the kitchen.

"Why don't you sit. I'll take this out of the oven."

He did as she said, and she could feel Carl's eyes on her from the doorway.

"Lacy, why are there police out back too?"

She looked toward him as she opened the oven. "We're just making sure everyone is safe, Vaughn."

She took the dish from the oven and set it on the stove. After studying the panel on the oven for a moment, she managed to turn it off.

"Are you comfortable?" she asked Vaughn when she turned and walked to the table.

"No. I'm surrounded by police. You're not saying anything. And I'm freaking out, Lacy. I'm freaking out."

"I know. I'm going to tell you why I'm here. First I'm going to ask if you have any weapons on you."

He narrowed his eyes on her. "I'm in my house. Why would I have a weapon? Look at what I'm wearing."

His point was valid. "Vaughn, Autumn was found dead this evening not far from where Stacy and Carley were found."

He didn't blink, but the bead of sweat on his lip hung there as he gasped for a breath, and then his hand came to his chest.

"Vaughn, are you okay? Talk to me." He nodded and sucked in another breath. "I'm going to get you a water. Don't move."

As she rose, Carl positioned himself to react if something should happen.

She pulled a glass from the cupboard nearest the sink and filled it. When she returned, she placed his hands around the glass. "Drink this."

With unsteady breath he lifted the glass to his lips and sipped.

When he'd calmed and his breathing returned with some normality, he looked her in the eye. "You think I killed Autumn?"

His voice was raw now, but she knew he was ready to talk.

"You were the last person anyone saw with her."

"No one saw us," he argued.

"I saw you."

He winced. "I would never hurt her. She's already hurt. That's why she wanted to come over. Lacy, her husband abuses her."

"Physically?"

"Mentally, and that's so much worse. She's a broken woman."

"You have to understand. You are known to have had relationships with our last three victims, and to have frequented the area where they were found. Vaughn, you're our only suspect."

He pressed his hand to his chest again. "I didn't do it. I have alibis for everywhere I've been. Lacy, you have to believe me."

"I have to take you in. If you're innocent, then you have nothing to worry about. And you'll be safe in our custody. If you're not who we're looking for, maybe you can think of someone we should look into. But if they're going after the women in your life, maybe your life is in danger."

"I'll go with you. I'm scared now, Lacy. I didn't do this to them. I swear."

"Okay, let's go." Vaughn and Lacy stood. "I'm going to handcuff you for your own safety, okay. You're not under arrest. This just keeps everyone from getting itchy."

Vaughn nodded and turned so that she could cuff his hands behind him.

Once outside, Lacy walked him to the squad car, and helped him inside. "I'll meet you at the station."

A few moments later, Lacy and Carl watched them drive away with Vaughn. "I need coffee," she growled.

"I can handle this. Go home."

"No way in hell."

"He's going to crack, Lacy. Let me make him talk."

She shook her head. "I'm not sure it's him."

"It leads to him."

"Not enough. We need the footage from his office. That building is wired, every inch of it. They'll have him going through the door, in the elevator, and working on whatever he was working on. He's had solid alibis for everything else, Moss. I think someone is trying to get to him."

"A husband?"

"Maybe. I think we need to question Autumn's husband. And we need to get some protection for Amy Cartwright and Olivia Burton."

"I can make that happen."

"Only problem is, if we send protection for them, it lets their secret out of the bag. Do you want to be the person that tells a whole family that their wife and or mother was cheating?"

"Christ, you make this hard," Carl rubbed the back of his neck. "Tomorrow we get to them, without their families, and tell them what we think."

"And they'll both be at Stacy's funeral. I can almost guarantee it."

"Then we'd better be there too."

14

D eclan felt like a stalker. He'd checked in on his brother-in-law and his parents, all of whom were fine. It was nearing ten o'clock and he'd driven by the parking lot near the wooded area they'd found his sister. Sure enough, there was plenty of police activity, but he didn't see Lacy's car.

A few more laps around the growing town he'd once called home, and he drove through the parking lot of the police station. Her car was parked there now. More work to be done, he supposed. But he'd have liked to have known she was safe and sound in her own home.

He shook his head and drove toward the exit. There was no mistake in his head that he was compensating.

Last week he was worked up over his ex-wife looking for more money from him. Then came his sister's death. Now he was trying to grab the reins on something and hold on tight before it all unraveled. Why he thought holding on to Lacy was the right thing to do, he'd never know. But it had him driving around at now ten-thirty at night wondering what she was working on.

Declan pulled up to the stop sign just as his phone rang.

Hoping it was Lacy, he answered it before even looking at the caller ID.

"Hello," he said, hearing the tremor in his voice.

"Dec, it's Vaughn. I need your help, man. I need a lawyer."

Now Declan pulled the phone from his ear and looked at the screen. It wasn't Vaughn's phone.

"Where are you?"

"I'm at the police station. They took me. I need you, man."

"I'll be right there."

He turned the car around and parked it right next to Lacy's.

CARL HAD BEEN A BABY ABOUT HER DRINKING HIS COKE, SO Lacy had bought two more from the vending machine. She was headed to the elevators when she saw Declan walk through the front doors of the station.

"What are you doing here?" she called to him and he hurried toward her as she pushed the button.

"Not taking the stairs?"

"I'm heading down, it's late, and I'm tired. So what?"

"Vaughn called me."

She pursed her lips and knew that Carl was done with his questioning.

"Why'd he call you?"

"Said he needed a lawyer."

"You're licensed in this state?"

"I'm... no."

"Don't see where you're going to be much help."

When the elevator door opened she stepped in and he followed. "What's he being held on?"

"You're not his lawyer."

"Lacy..."

"Listen, Matthews, this is a mess. I don't need you stepping in and..."

He moved into her and pressed his lips to hers. Shoving him back, she swiped at her mouth with the back of her hand, the Coke still held tightly in her fingertips.

"What was that for?"

"I'm not going to let you snap in and out of cop mode. You have a job to do, fine. You have my friend in custody, fine. But damnit, you and I had a thing going, and it was leading to something potentially nice. So I'm going to remind you that I'd like to finish that up some day and see where it goes."

"It's not going anywhere. You live on Central Park West, remember? I live here."

The door opened and she stepped out and into the dimly lit hallway less enhanced with green speckled flooring that was as old as the building.

She ran her name badge in front of the door scanner and it clicked to unlock. Declan quickly moved in front of her to open it for her.

"One of those Cokes for me?" he asked.

"You'll have to arm wrestle Moss for it. He's whining because I drank his other one."

She walked down another depressing hallway and stopped before another locked door. "I shouldn't let you in here," she said. "You're not licensed in this state."

"He's scared, Lacy. You can tell."

"I know he is. And to tell you the truth, I only have him here for his own protection." She thought for a moment about Declan's lack of licensure, and realized she'd never asked a lawyer about their credentials before. Who's to say she asked this time. So she decided to fill him in, but because of Stacy, she needed to ease him in.

Declan stepped in closer to her. "Why his protection?"

She looked at the door, and then at the room across the hall. "C'mon, let's talk."

Lacy handed him the Cokes, unlocked the door, and stepped inside.

The room was more depressing than the hallway, and meant to be. No two-way glass, like on TV. Just a camera in each corner of the room. Nothing was secret in that building.

She pulled out one of the old metal chairs and sat down, expecting Declan to do the same, but he stood in the doorway with a Coke in each hand.

"Come sit down and I'll let you have one," she offered.

"I don't drink Coke."

"Then why give me a hard time about it?"

"Just felt right." He set the Cokes on the table, then eased himself onto the table looking down at her. "You're about to tell me something I don't want to hear. I've been in this situation enough times. I pace when I take in information and process it. So, I'm not going to sit in a chair."

Okay, she'd been warned, so she stood, because she didn't like talking up to people. And wouldn't you know it, she needed to pace too.

"I brought Vaughn in under the umbrella of suspicion for the murder of Autumn Taylor."

"Why is he a suspect?"

"One, he was having an affair with her. Two, he was with her at the funeral home before her murder. Three, when we got to his house he was waiting for her."

"Then it doesn't sound like he killed her, does it?"

"He had an affair with a previous victim who died the same way in the same area."

"Carley?"

"Yes." She wondered if he knew about Stacy the way he pulled Carley's name out of memory so quickly.

Now he paced with his hands tucked into the pockets of his suit pants.

There was pain shadowing his face and his lips twitched

before he pursed them tightly. "Vaughn has affairs with married women. It's common knowledge."

"Yes."

"And they're turning up dead."

"Yes."

He turned to her, his eyes glossy with the threat of tears. "Lace, we have three victims."

"Yes."

Locking his eyes with hers, he took a deep breath. "Vaughn was having an affair with my sister?"

She found that when he'd taken a breath she'd began to hold hers, so she let it escape in a sigh, but it didn't release the tension she'd felt gripping her body tightly. "Declan, I'm so sorry."

He squeezed his eyes shut and turned toward the wall, away from her. She watched his shoulders rise and fall as he took calming deep breaths. But a moment later he turned and slammed his fist down on the old wooden table. She jumped back toward the door as he shook his hand from the evident pain it had caused.

"What the hell, Matthews?"

"I'm pissed."

"I see that. Need a punching bag? I'll get you one. Don't you dare try to use me for it. I'll kick your ass."

"You think I'd hit you?" His voice rose.

"No, I'm just warning you."

"And I'm warning you to back off and let me have a moment." He turned away again, nursing his hand.

She gave him a few minutes to pace the room and gather the composure he needed.

When he turned back to her, the calm had returned. She supposed it was something he could control in his line of work, much as she could.

"I'll get you some ice for that hand," she offered.

"It'll be fine until I get home." He looked down at his

bloodied knuckles, and opened and closed his hand into a fist. "Does Tom know about this? I mean, I assume you have to tell him things like this, right?"

"We didn't tell him about the affair. Vaughn has solid alibis for the past two murders." She saw him wince at the word. "It looks like he's solidly accounted for here too. We got to Autumn maybe only twenty minutes after she died. Whoever did it is right in the area, Declan. We have to assume everyone is a suspect at this point. But his association with the victims puts him top of the list."

"Except he wasn't around for them."

"Except that."

He shook his head and gripped the sides of the table. "I can't believe Stacy..." He closed his eyes tightly again and took a moment. "What makes women do that? Women with husbands and kids? I don't understand."

She didn't understand it either, and she was one of those kids who was glad she'd never known until she was older—and even then she didn't understand it.

"For whatever reason she did it, I know she loved Tom and the kids. I guess she just needed more."

His narrow gaze met hers. "You were friends. She never told you about it?"

"Never. I had no idea at all."

"But we have to assume that it's why she's dead and so are the other two. Someone knew. Someone knew Vaughn was having these affairs with these women."

"And we know the names of a couple more and we're going to get them some protection."

He shook his head again. "There are more? What the hell is wrong with him?"

"He thought he was helping them."

"Maybe he should be in jail."

"Can't hold him for that."

"But you're not stopping with him, right?"

"Of course not. Tom will be questioned again as well as Carley's husband and Autumn's. We're going to find the person responsible."

"I know you will." He stood up straight, flexed his hand, and took another deep breath. "Okay, let me see Vaughn."

"You really want to do that?"

"I'm professional, Lacy. I can talk to people I think are piles of crap and still be professional."

"He's still your friend. Don't give up on him. He needs you right now."

"Yeah, well I don't know how I feel about him in a friendship sort of way."

She nodded. That was understandable. "I'll let you talk to him if you promise to keep your head about you."

His nostrils flared. "I promise."

❧ 15 ❧

Lacy opened the door to the room, where Vaughn waited, very slowly. She was judging the mood of the man in the hallway against the man in the room.

Carl stood from his chair in the corner when she entered and Vaughn lifted his head, his hands remained on the table. His eyes widened when he saw Declan walk in behind her.

"Oh, Dec. I'm glad you're here, man. I didn't do this," Vaughn began his pleading. "Tell them I didn't do this."

Declan turned to look Lacy. "Can I have a few minutes with my client?"

What would it hurt she thought. "Yeah. We have eyes on the room."

"No doubt."

She gave Carl a nod toward the door. He eyed both Vaughn and Declan, then followed her to the hall. "Did you get the info from the office building yet?"

"Haven't looked. I'm sure we have the footage by now. We'll have to let him go when his alibi checks out."

"They agreed to park a car outside his house."

"Good. We need to question Autumn Taylor's husband."

He gave her a nod. "Can't wait. Had a run in with him a few years back. DUI."

"Fantastic." She pinched the bridge of her nose. "Can't think of any better way to start the day. Looking at her watch she groaned. "I might as well get a pot of coffee and keep going."

Carl laughed. "It's been a long day. Why don't you go home and get some sleep."

"What about you?"

"I went home earlier and accidentally took a nap."

"Accidentally?"

He laughed. "Turned on the Flash. My DVR was full and I needed to catch up. Ten minutes in and I was sound asleep. Looks like I'll have to catch up later."

The door to the room opened and Declan stepped out. "Did you get footage from security cameras from when Vaughn was at his office?"

"I was heading up to my desk to check my email. Wish to join me?" she asked.

"Yeah. He says it'll prove he was there, just like he said he was."

Carl moved to the door. "I'll sit with him. What about that Coke you promised me?"

"It's in the other room. I'll be back down in a few minutes." She started down the long depressing hallway with Declan a few steps behind. She led them through the door and down to the elevator. When it opened, they stepped inside.

"There'll be a few more witnesses to his location during the murder," Declan offered as he watched the numbers on the elevator count up.

"I know he talked to the security guard."

"Yep, and of course the phone log will show he called for some technical support on the server he was fixing."

"That'll be helpful."

"And if you find Crystal Bradley, she just might crack too."

"And who is Crystal Bradley?"

"Perhaps the one and only single woman Vaughn is sleeping with."

The doors opened and Lacy stepped out and turned to Declan. "He was with her in that time?"

"She met him in the office and they had fifteen minutes in the ladies room. Office was empty, but he's sure the cameras would see them going in and coming out."

Lacy shook her head. "I don't know if he's a lucky S.O.B. or disgusting."

"Fine line," he said as she walked toward her desk and sat down.

"Let's hope it's all there. I have a gut feeling that Vaughn isn't our guy and we might just be wasting our time."

"I'm no detective, but I'm guessing you've concluded that he, too, might be in danger if someone is targeting these women."

"Yes. When he's released he'll have protection."

"Good."

She turned on her computer and found the email she'd been looking for. Declan moved in behind her and leaned in as they watched Vaughn enter the building, ride the elevator, walk through the cubicles and into the room where the computer server was housed. He made a phone call, did some work, and did some kind a dance while he waited for the computer to prompt him.

"The things we do when we think no one is looking," Declan joked.

She chuckled and continued watching as Vaughn logged off the computer, turned off the light, and then watched as Crystal Bradley walked toward him and then wrapped herself around him as they kissed for what seemed like eternity while Lacy watched it. Then, just as Vaughn had said, hand in hand they went into the ladies room. Fifteen minutes later they both walked out and Crystal adjusted the skirt that she had on.

Lacy's stomach lurched a bit. Vaughn was nothing but a huge male slut. Maybe she was jealous. It had been months since she'd had sex, and it had been as casual. Sometimes it paid to have a friend with benefits in another state.

Declan stood straight. "According to the timestamp, Vaughn was right where he said he was at the time of the murder."

"Looks like he's innocent."

Declan moved from behind her, and stood on the other side of the desk. He scrubbed his hands over his face. "I assume you'll be a few more hours here?"

She checked her watch and noticed that it was already past midnight. "For a little while longer, I guess."

"Someone will walk you and your gun to the car?"

She smiled. "Yes. I'll be fine."

"I have to go home. Tomorrow is going to be the day from hell."

Lacy stood. "I'm going to try to be there, but..."

"I'd rather you find the piece of shit that did it."

She nodded. "I will."

"I know you will."

They stood in silence for a moment before he moved to her. Raising his hand to her cheek, he pulled her near, and pressed his warm lips to hers. "I'm staying in town until this is settled. I want some time with you."

"Declan, I don't know how to feel about all this. I don't want it to cloud my position on this case."

"It doesn't cloud it at all. You have a job and you're focused on it. This is about us, Lace. We didn't get to finish this fifteen years ago. I mean, a few times in the back of my car wasn't a relationship."

"You're looking for a relationship?"

"I'm looking to feel this out." He held his finger under her chin and locked his gaze with hers. "I never forgot about you, Lace. Never."

She couldn't explain how it warmed her to hear that. But the fact that he'd someday leave again, that only broke her heart.

He dropped his hand and started for the elevators. After he pushed the button, he turned back. "You're probably going to be looking at the camera downstairs from my time with Vaughn."

"There's no audio."

"Yeah, well, you won't need it. But when you see Vaughn's eye, you'll know I told him I found out about him with my sister." He smiled as the door opened. "We're cool now, but I'll probably kick his ass over it again." He was still smiling when the door closed.

Because she couldn't help herself, she sat back down at her computer and logged into the cameras. She watched as Declan walked into the room and a sobbing Vaughn began to rise. She couldn't make out the words said between them, but they were obviously heated. Then there was the moment Declan pulled back and popped Vaughn right in the eye. She stifled the laugh that wanted to burst free. "Good for you, Declan. Good for you."

❧ 16 ❧

Declan looked in the mirror over the bathroom sink, and adjusted his tie. Angie had sent his things as he'd asked her to do. And she picked his nicest ties. When he'd checked in with her the day before, she'd said that the office had taken up a collection for flowers. She'd asked for the address of the church. She was a good assistant and friend. He didn't have many friends—not really. She was as close as it came.

As he shrugged on his suit jacket, and took the lint roller to it, he gave some thought to his life in New York. The view from his bedroom window was priceless. The suit he wore was nearly two thousand dollars, and custom made. The watch on his arm was a Rolex. Did any of that matter? Most nights, dinner was carryout from somewhere near his condo. Companionship of a nice woman wasn't very often had either, but usually if he asked for a dinner date, he could get one.

But here, where he was raised, he had people. His parents were getting older now, and Stacy wouldn't be there to take care of them. And what about her kids? They needed to be around his family so that her memory wouldn't be lost.

He looked at the bloodshot, tired eyes in the mirror looking back at him. Everything he'd ever wanted, he had in New York. When had he decided he didn't want a family? Vaughn was a son-of-a-bitch that he would punch in the face at least one more time for having an affair with his sister, but he'd been a friend. And Declan was smart enough to understand that it took two to tango. Something deeper must have been going on with his sister to have her turn to Vaughn. If he stayed around, maybe he could find out what that was.

The knock on the bathroom door had him snapping out of his sorrowful mood. He opened the door to see his mother standing there in a dress he hadn't seen since he was a child. And if he remembered correctly, Stacy had had a matching one.

"Mom, you look lovely," he said moving in and kissing her on the cheek.

"And you sure do clean up nice," she said patting his cheek. "The car has arrived."

"I'll be right down."

She gave him a nod and headed for the stairs. Declan wondered if she'd taken some of those pills the hospital had given her, just to get through the day. Of all days, he assumed she'd be a wreck, and she looked to be functioning just fine.

One more look in the mirror, and he decided that he looked good enough to accept the condolences of the people he'd left behind. How could anyone face a day that they knew would be filled with complete sadness. There simply wasn't any good to come from the day, he thought. If his mother didn't end up back in the hospital, he'd be surprised.

His parents waited at the bottom of the staircase for him. Without another word between them, they walked out to the family car. A different car would pick up Tom, the kids, and his parents. He knew that his insides were absolutely twisted up, he couldn't even imagine how Stacy's children were going to make it through the day. Declan was grateful that Tom's parents had come to be with them. Tom was surely going to be a lost soul without Stacy.

⚜

LACY SLAMMED HER CAR DOOR OUTSIDE THE CHURCH. THE parking lot was packed, and she and Carl had parked across the street.

"You know that a full funeral means you were too damn young to die," he said as they both buttoned up their jackets.

"She was."

"Did you bring your ice pack for your eye?" he asked as she slipped on her sunglasses.

"I'll be fine for an hour. Damned son-of-a-bitch. No wonder Autumn Taylor was messing around on her husband."

"I told you he was a piece of work."

"And now he's a piece of work sitting in a jail cell. You don't get away with punching a *bitch cop*," she quoted him using her fingers as air quotes.

They walked toward the church, and she scoped out the area. There were the obvious, to her, unmarked cars in the lot. They'd set up four undercover officers to attend the funeral, and they'd do the same for Autumn's funeral as well. Often the person who would kill would attend a funeral. It was sick, but it was how they thought. And now that there were three victims, she was sure it was a serial killer, and that made her sick.

Carl opened the door to the church for her, and she walked through to the full sanctuary. The casket was closed in the front, and Lacy wondered if that was for the kids. She'd never forget what it was like to sit at her mother's funeral and look at her.

She slid into the last pew, and Carl sat next to her. She acknowledged the undercover officers, and took a moment to scan the room herself. Most of the mourners were looking forward. She was searching for the person scanning the room, much as she was.

"Maybe you should take your sunglasses off," Carl whispered to her.

"No way. I'm fine."

Lacy continued her scan of the room. When she noticed Amy Cartwright and her husband in the sixth pew on the other side of the church, she realized that one of the undercover officers was seated only a few feet away. They were watching her, and that's what Lacy had wanted. When she could ensure that Amy wasn't with her husband, Lacy would talk to her. She looked around, and was surprised that Olivia Burton, Pastor Ralph's wife wasn't at the funeral. He'd told Lacy that she was sick. She must have had something that had her in bed. She'd never known Olivia Burton to miss a funeral or wedding.

Pastor Ralph read scripture and talked about Stacy and her contribution to the community. Mourners dabbed their eyes, and sobs could be heard.

Lacy caught sight of Declan in the front pew, his arm draped around the shoulder of his sobbing mother. Tom had his daughter on his lap, her head rested on his shoulder, and his son wrapped under his other arm.

Anger had heat creeping up the back of Lacy's neck. A family had been destroyed. Multiple families. Three victims. It went past just husbands and children. There were siblings to those women, parents, and friends. Someone was ruining a community, and she was going to see it end.

Carl nudged Lacy, and she noticed he was standing, as was the congregation. She hurried to her feet.

Pastor Ralph led the congregation in prayer, and then each row filed out of the pews and past the family. This was the part of the day she dreaded. She and Carl could just go right back out the door and disappear, but she felt as though she needed to pay her respects as well.

She watched as each pew emptied out. The other officers had made their way through the line as well, saying something along the lines of them being friends or just giving condolences. It was easy enough to blend into funerals. The mourning didn't question much.

As she approached, she caught Declan's eye. The corner of his mouth lifted in a smile, and her heart squeezed.

Lacy hugged Tom, and each of the kids. She shook the hand of Declan's father and held his mother when she began to sob. As she moved from Declan's mother, he held his hand out to her and she reached for it. The squeeze he gave her fingers sent a jolt straight to her heart. When he pulled her near, he leaned in to her ear and whispered, "Are you undercover? What's with the sunglasses?"

"Not even going there, Matthews."

He pulled back and studied her before leaning in again. "I'm coming to your house tonight. I'll be there at seven. We're having dinner, and I'll bring it."

"Demanding, aren't you, Matthews?"

He lifted his brows and then his eyes grew serious again. "I need you."

Lacy bit down hard on her bottom lip hearing the word *need* come from his lips. She gave his hand a squeeze, just as he'd done to her, and then she moved on.

Walking back to the car, she kept a steady pace ahead of Carl. When she'd opened the door, she slid in behind the steering wheel and reached for the ice bag she'd left there. Lifting her sunglasses to the top of her head, she placed it on her eye as Carl climbed into the car.

"In a hurry, Pratt?" he asked, as he situated himself.

"This isn't cold anymore," she groaned, tossing the ice pack into the floor behind her seat. "Sorry. Funerals make me—crazy."

"Why don't you take the rest of the day off," he offered. "Stacy was a friend. It's more than a case to you."

"I'm fine. We have an agenda."

"And our agenda already got you punched in the face."

Lacy chuckled. "It's been a long time since I've been hit."

"I'm sure he feels worse. You had him on the ground before he knew what hit him. Cuffed and cussing."

"All in a day's work."

Lacy pulled away from the curb and headed toward the Starbucks where Stacy had worked. She wanted to read the staff. There were a few at the funeral that she recognized, but she wanted to get a feel for those who hadn't gone. And she wanted a coffee—a huge, extra caffeinated, full of sugar, cup of coffee.

❧ 17 ❧

Perhaps everyone had filtered out of the funeral and headed to Starbucks, Lacy thought as she watched the door continually open and close. The people walking in were people she'd recognized as those who were honoring Stacy. Perhaps this was part of the ritual.

A young man behind the counter took orders, but she noticed that he lifted his glasses often to wipe his tearing eyes. Obviously, he was touched by what had happened to Stacy.

"You could see better if you took your sunglasses off," Carl poked at her as he sipped his coffee.

"Not ready for that yet."

"Detective Pratt?" A woman's voice detoured her stare and she looked up to see Amy Cartwright standing next to her. "My name is Amy Cartwright."

"Yes, Ms. Cartwright, I know who you are. How can I help you?"

"Stacy's brother told me I should find you. He said you wanted to talk to me." Amy scanned a look over the store. "About Vaughn Price," she whispered.

"Yes," Lacy agreed and pulled her sunglasses off, realizing she probably did seem even more standoffish than normal. She noticed Amy wince when she saw the red swollen skin that had been concealed. "Not everyone likes cops," she joked as Amy nodded.

Carl stood. "Ms. Cartwright, can I get you a coffee?"

"I'd like that. Just a vanilla latte if you don't mind."

He walked to the counter and Lacy motioned to Amy to have a seat. "We would appreciate a moment of your time."

"I don't know if I should talk to you here. There's a lot of people. But I do want to tell you that I'm scared."

"Why?"

"I'm not stupid, even if I feel that way. But I know Vaughn dates married women. I know I'm not the only one that has a thing for him."

A thing. Lacy couldn't imagine what that thing was as she surely didn't see the attraction. Maybe it was because she wasn't married.

Amy clasped her hands atop the table. "My husband and I have been married for eight years. We've hit a dry spell—a boring plateau I guess you could say. I thought he was having an affair with a co-worker. Instead of confronting him, I thought I'd do something irrational too. So I went out one night, drinking with some friends, and I met Vaughn. I didn't think it would really happen or become anything." Her voice was still a whisper.

"How long ago was this?"

"Six, no eight months ago. I thought, oh just this one time, this one night, but..." She sucked in a breath. "I became obsessed. The man is a god at making a woman feel something she forgot she could feel."

Lacy pushed back her coffee. The thought of Vaughn touching a woman made her sick. Especially after seeing the footage of him and Crystal Bradley making out before ducking into the ladies room.

Amy lifted her eyes to meet Lacy's. "Detective Pratt, I'm not some slut. I swear. It just happened."

It happened because she let it happen, Lacy thought, but she had a case to solve and that didn't include casting judgement on Amy. "Your husband's affair?"

Amy shook her head. "He wasn't having one. It was a huge misunderstanding."

"And you told him about you and Vaughn?"

Amy's eyes grew wide and she shook her head again. "Oh, no. No, I couldn't. He'd leave. But I did call it off with Vaughn. I told him I wanted to fix my marriage and he was okay with it. He understood."

Carl returned with Amy's coffee, and set it down in front of her. He exchanged a glance with Lacy. "I'm going to go talk to some of the employees. The young man named Carter is taking it pretty hard. I'll see what he has to say."

"Thanks," Lacy said, and then turned back to Amy as Carl walked away. "What did you do then?"

"I got counseling. I went to the church and talked to Pastor Ralph about what I'd done. Other than you, he's the only person I told. I'm ashamed of what I did. But grateful for it too. Does that make sense?"

Lacy wasn't sure it did make sense. Adultery was something she'd never be able to wrap her head around. "So why are you telling me all of this?"

"Declan said that you'd taken Vaughn in as a suspect in Stacy's murder. I didn't know he and Stacy..." She stopped picked up her coffee and sipped. "I guess we all have issues, don't we?"

Lacy sat quietly and watched Amy process her statement.

Amy sat her cup down. "I knew he was sleeping with Autumn. I'd gone to his house one night in desperation, and she was walking out. They'd kissed one of those after sex kind of kisses. I got jealous, real jealous. I drove around for a few hours while my husband was sleeping. And I drove right back to Vaughn's house with the intent to give him a piece of my mind, but instead..."

Lacy figured Amy knew she didn't need the details. "I assume you're seeing the pattern we are then. Someone is killing the married women Vaughn has had relationships with."

Amy nodded. "I don't think it's Vaughn though. No one can have that much compassion and kill someone."

"He has solid alibis for the times of the murders. He's being kept safe too."

"But I might be in danger."

"We believe you are. We'd like to have some protection for you, but that would entail you telling your husband."

"I can't do that."

"It's your decision, Amy. But you need to know that we don't think the other three women were killed by a stranger. They were obviously comfortable with the person."

"Oh," she said as she let out a sigh. "I guess I was expecting some violent person who maybe jumped them, or broke into their house."

"It might be easier that way. You could be more prepared for something like that." Lacy gripped her cup. "Are you sure your husband didn't know about your affair?"

"I'm sure," she answered quickly. "Why?"

"If he knew, maybe he's holding a grudge against Vaughn."

"Do you mean he's a suspect?"

"At this point everyone is. But he would have motive. Then again, you would too."

"Me?"

"Sure, maybe you're jealous of all the other women."

"No. I wouldn't do something like that. Stacy and Carley have kids. You don't take a mother from her kids."

You don't cheat on your spouse either, Lacy wanted to remind her, but she kept quiet.

"The way I see it, you can either tell your husband all of this so he knows we're looking into him. Or you can tell me where he was when the other murders happened."

"I always know where he is."

"Are you sure?"

"Yes." Amy sipped her coffee. "He works from home. He logs into his computer all the time. And when I thought he was having an affair, I put one of those trackers on his car. You know the ones you can buy for teen drivers? It tells me where he's at all the time." She pulled out her iPhone, and opened the app. "See, right now he's at the YMCA working out. I told him I was going for coffee, and he said he was going to work out after the funeral."

Lacy texted the information to one of the officers that had been following the Cartwrights at the funeral. He confirmed that he was at the YMCA working out, alone, earbuds in, and that the man was a machine.

"Can you send me that information?" Lacy asked.

"Yes." Amy pressed a few things and then asked for Lacy's email. A moment later her phone alerted her that she'd received the information. She also provided information so they could check his logins from his computer.

Lacy pulled a business card from her pocket and handed it to Amy.

"Keep your eyes open. Let me know if you need anything or if you think of anything that might help us."

Lacy picked up her cup and walked out of the store with Carl. She slid on her sunglasses and headed to the car. As they climbed in, she rested her cup in the holder, and started the engine.

"Cartwright has a tracker on her husband's car. One of those things you put in a teenager's car," she explained. "We should be able to see if he drove near the trail at all during those days."

"Helpful."

"What did you find out?"

"That Carter Workman, barista, was infatuated with Stacy Watts. I mean stalker infatuated."

"No kidding?" she asked as she pulled out of the parking lot.

"He was a little choked up when I talked to him. But he knew her schedule as well as he knew his name. Maybe even better. He had pictures on his phone of her at work and in the community. They spent a lot of time together, but I think that was his design. Someone else," he looked at the notes he'd taken on his phone, "Chase Martinez, said Workman would follow Stacy home if she was there after dark. Usually she worked school hours, but not always."

"There was a big age difference between Workman and Stacy."

"Thirteen years. I thought that too."

"Mother figure for him?"

Carl shook his head. "Mrs. Robinson?"

Lacy laughed. "Mrs. Robinson seduced. Do you think that's what Stacy did?"

"No. I think she was just kind to him."

As Lacy turned into the parking lot of the police station, she nodded in agreement. "But if Workman knew about her affair with Vaughn, he might have had a jealous thing going on?"

"The manager showed me schedules. Workman was at the counter at the time of Stacy's death. He told me he's been a blubbering idiot since they learned what happened. He said he's tried to send him home numerous times, but the kid wants to work."

"The alibis win again. We're missing another common thread between our victims, other than Vaughn."

"Let's go up and hash it out. Unless you'd like to head home. You look like shit."

Ah, he was always good with the compliments, Lacy thought. "I've got some more steam in me. Let's get to work."

❧ 18 ❧

eclan's mother had finally taken one of those pills that they'd given her at the hospital to make her sleep. She'd been resting for an hour already, and he was sure he wouldn't see her until the next morning. The funeral had emptied her, and he thought that was for the best. Perhaps she could begin on reaching some closure. Though, he knew she'd never have that completely, maybe when Lacy had someone locked up, she'd have a little peace.

His father had retreated out to the garage where he had a dozen projects in various stages of repair. Declan poured two glasses of iced tea from the refrigerator and headed out to sit with his father.

At the moment, his father was working on an old lawn mower. Why, Declan didn't understand. There was a new one sitting there, but his father must have seen some value in it.

"I brought you a drink," he said to get his father's attention.

"Oh, thanks." He turned to collect it from Declan. "What are your plans? Are you heading back to New York soon?"

Declan sat on the small set of stairs that led from the house to the garage as his father went back to his work bench, took a sip of tea, and then set it to the side.

"No. I'm staying until I know you and mom are okay and they find the person responsible." He paused for a moment. "You know that they found another victim last night."

Without turning around his father said, "I heard something about it."

"It's too close, and I want to see it finished. They took Vaughn in for questioning yesterday," he said, and then wished he hadn't.

His father turned. "Why Vaughn?"

"He had relationships with some of the victims."

His father nodded and turned back to his work. Obviously not worried that one of those relationships was with his daughter.

"His alibis all check out," Declan continued. "He wasn't around for any of them."

"Some sick bastard out there is."

"Yeah."

Declan still couldn't decide why it brought him some comfort that the victims weren't injured or raped. They were still dead.

"I'm going to go out tonight. Will you and Mom be okay?"

"She'll be asleep. And that nosy neighbor Mrs. Clancy filled the fridge. I have plenty to eat and all. We'll be fine."

Declan stood. "If you need me, you call me. I'll be in town."

"Seeing the detective?"

Declan laughed. "What makes you say that?"

His father shrugged. "I saw you talk to her today. Looked more than friendly."

"We dated in high school. Do you remember that?"

"I just remember that she was the girl that moved here after her mother was killed. She took an interest in you."

It was funny what his father remembered. "Yeah, well, we're going to have dinner."

"Are you trying to play lawyer and get your nose in her investigation?"

"No. Just seeing if there's still a spark."

His father turned and narrowed his gaze at him. "There's a spark. I saw it."

Declan held in the chuckle that tried to surface. "I'll let you know."

LACY'S HEAD POUNDED. HER EYE WAS FREAKING SORE AS HELL. Why had she agreed to Declan coming over, she wondered as she pulled off her shirt and tossed it into the laundry. And was she supposed to open the door for him wearing her sweats and a tank top, which was what she wanted to put on. Or was he expecting something *more comfortable?*

Her mood grew gloomier the more she looked in her closet and saw nothing but white button down shirts, or ratty T-shirts. No doubt he'd show up in some businessman looking thing and she'd feel unimpressive.

She reached for a cotton dress with bold flowers, more suited for summer than fall, that simply hung on her body. It wasn't dressy, it wasn't a pair of sweatpants either. Sliding it over her body, she looked in the mirror. Oh hell, she looked like she was heading out to play tennis, and her eye was turning purple. Lovely.

The doorbell stopped her from berating herself further. Quickly, she ran her fingers through her hair to give it a bit of volume and headed to the front door in her bare feet, which she now noted needed a pedicure.

Lacy pulled open the door, and there he stood. Declan Matthews, no longer the teenager she'd had etched in her mind for the past fifteen years, but the man, his eyes hollow from grief.

"Wow," he said as he blinked hard. "Not what I expected you to look like tonight."

"Don't give me grief. I don't know how to do this."

"Do what? Have dinner? We've eaten together every day since I got here. I think you do fine with that."

"That's not what I meant."

A sexy smile formed on his lips and her insides instantly warmed. Then it faded, and he lifted his hand to her cheek.

"What the hell happened to you?"

Lacy jerked back. "Part of the job."

"Bullshit. Who did that to you?"

"Someone I was questioning. He might have had a solid alibi for the reason I was questioning him, but he's in jail now for assaulting an officer of the law."

Declan stepped closer to her and pressed a gentle kiss to the bruise. "That's why you wore the sunglasses?"

"I'll put them back on if you make a big deal about this."

"I'm done, but I'm mad."

"Nothing you could do about it." She looked at the bag he carried. "What did you bring?"

"Gyros."

She lifted her brows. "Gyros? Where'd you go to get those?"

"Forty miles. I seriously had to drive forty miles to find them. I had a craving. I have one or three a week in New York."

She eased and stepped back so he could walk through the door. "Straight back to the kitchen," she said, noting he was in a pair of nicely fitted jeans, and a crisp new T-shirt. But still as sexy as he'd been in that expensive suit.

Declan set the bag on the counter. "I didn't think to stop for something to go with it. Wine or beer."

Lacy frowned. "You might be out of luck. I don't stock much food or drink here." She opened the refrigerator. "I have three beers, all different kinds, four Cokes, and a bottle of wine Carl and his wife gave me for Christmas. Never opened."

"Let's open the wine," he said as he pulled cartons from the bag. "I could seriously use some wine."

Lacy pulled the wine from the fridge and turned to look at

him as she closed the door. "I'm sorry you had to go through all that today. No one should ever have to bury their loved ones under those circumstances."

"I appreciate that." He carried the containers to the table. "My mom finally took some sleeping pills, so she's resting. Dad is in his garage fixing stuff. Tom straight up told me he was going home, locking himself in his bedroom, and drinking until he passed out."

Lacy moved to him, setting the wine on the table. "That's not a good plan."

"Sounded solid to me."

"I guess everyone deals with the grief differently."

Declan took her hand and spun her to him. The moment she was pressed against his chest, she lifted her arms around his neck, and his hands gripped her waist. "I plan to drown my sorrows in you," he said, his voice a hungry growl.

Lacy leapt at his mouth and took it. There was no more control, or compassion—only heat and need. She was done thinking that she should be professional. The detective should separate from the victim, but she couldn't. It was all too personal.

She hadn't felt whole since the last time Declan held her close to him. Now his hands skimmed down her thighs and wandered back up under the skirt, against her skin.

She gasped at his touch, breaking the kiss, only to have his mouth come to her throat with that heated tongue stroking her skin.

Declan's hands traveled under the dress to her breasts, and he cupped them, sending a pulse through her that throbbed with a need she could no longer control. Slipping his thumb under the fabric of her bra, he pressed against the tender skin of her nipple, and a moan escaped her as her knees grew weak. Would he take her if she collapsed to the floor? What would be left of her if he took her further than just a kiss or a touch.

His hands pulled at the dress until he lifted it over her head.

Suddenly she was thankful for the choice she'd made. Somehow she'd managed to lift her eyes to meet his. The blue dreaminess had been replaced with a darkness that made Declan look possessed—by her.

He ripped at her bra until her breasts were freed, and latched his hot mouth around them, tugging at her nipple with his teeth.

Her hands fought to grip tightly enough to stand, her hips now pressed against the table behind her.

Declan's hand wandered down her stomach, his fingers skimming the top of her panties, and then they slipped down under the fabric until he cupped her and she threw her head back.

"Here or your bed? I'm not going to last much longer," he implored, as his voice deepened with need.

"Here. I don't want to wait," she pleaded as he pulled her panties from her hips, shoved her up onto the table, and started for the button on his jeans.

Lacy gripped the edge of the table as she watched him free himself, realizing she'd never actually seen his body. Their sexual escapades of youth were in dark corners where no one would see, including themselves.

As his jeans bunched to the floor Declan gripped her hips, pulled her to his erection, and the plea that had formed hissed out, "Yes."

Without restraint, he dove into her, filling her physically and emotionally. With each thrust she gripped him. Remembering that it was this that had made her once feel whole when she was broken. This, which now, made her want to hold on, to keep him near.

He buried his face in her neck, and Lacy gripped the fabric of his shirt just to hold on as the release that built between them grew and grew.

The words *I love you* stuck in her throat. It wasn't a new sensation, just because his mouth was on her neck, his hands on her body, and he moved inside her. They'd always been there. He'd always been that important but she wasn't going to say them.

His fingers dug into delicate skin, and she wanted to cry out, but the pain was glorious. He needed her, just as she needed him. It might only be for now, or maybe a few more glorious nights if they could manage it, but he'd be gone. As his breath shuddered, and his grip grew firmer, she knew she needed desperately to hold on to this moment and capture it.

When his body thrust once more, and his muscles shook, he held her as close as he possibly could. That climb they'd taken together had them both gasping for breath, and panting each other's names.

Declan slid his fingers into her hair and took her mouth again. "God, Lacy. That was incredible."

"It was," she huffed out a breath and gasped for another. "I've never used my table like that before."

He chuckled against her throat. "I have to stand here for a moment. My legs are shaking."

"Next time the bed. Then you won't have to go anywhere after."

Declan eased back and locked eyes with her. Perhaps he would protest the offer, but a smile formed on his sexy mouth. "I like the sound of that."

❦ 19 ❦

Once they'd caught their breath, Lacy went to her room to change. This time, she was opting for the sweats and T-shirt she'd wanted to wear in the first place. There had been a moment's contemplation of framing that dress. God, she'd never felt as relaxed and as fulfilled as she did at that moment. And it had been Declan that had brought her that euphoric bliss.

She could hear him in her kitchen, opening drawers and cupboard doors. It occurred to her that she'd never had a man in her house—ever. What a pathetic life she lived. She was all work —all the time. No wonder she'd had to go out of state to have a weekend of sex with a friend.

And it occurred to her at that moment, this was what women saw in Vaughn Price. They needed that release they weren't getting at home—including Stacy.

Declan was sitting at the table when she returned. He'd removed his shoes and socks, and his T-shirt. His jeans had been pulled up, but the button was left undone.

"I got hot," he said winking as she walked through the door.

"I'll put my shirt back on if you want me too. Both my mother and my ex-wife preferred shirts on at the table.

"Keep it off," she instructed as she passed by him and ran her fingers across his back from shoulder to shoulder. "It occurred to me, in the middle of our little tangle, I'd never seen you naked."

"Sure you have. We had sex more than once."

Smiling, she sat down at the chair next to him. "It was always in your car, in the dark, under a blanket. And yes, we had sex more than once. Six times to be exact. No, now it's seven."

He grinned before he pursed his lips. "You know how many times we were together?"

"If I look real hard I could probably find the diary where I detailed it and the dates."

He reached for her hand and pressed a kiss to her fingers. "That is the sexiest thing any woman has ever said to me."

"Don't consider it sexy. If you read the entries you'd be saddened."

Declan wrapped both his hands around her one, lacing his fingers around hers. "Why would I be?"

"I told you, I felt as though I used you. I needed that acceptance to deal with life without a mother, and a manic depressive father. You gave it to me."

"So me coming here tonight needing you flipped things a bit?"

"I wasn't thinking of it like that. I just…" She sat back in her seat. "I guess so."

He scooted his chair closer to her. "I've had a lot of sex in my life," he said and she swallowed the lump that formed in her throat. "I've never had sex that mind-blowing."

"You're just saying that."

Taking her chin, he directed her to his mouth where she could taste the wine he'd drunk. "I'm not just saying it. You rocked my world fifteen years ago. You rocked it tonight."

"And what are we going to do when you move back home?"

He eased back. "We'll think about it then. They have lawyers here and cops there. We can work it out. For tonight, let's eat gyros. Let's drink wine. Let's get naked and have more sex. And if you want to see me naked, we could keep the lights on."

The smile that formed on her lips was genuine. She wanted to embrace this while it lasted. It was easy for her to tarnish it and make it horrible. She could do that without much thought. It would take more work to enjoy him while he was here with her, and she wanted to enjoy every sensual, heartfelt, wild moment he was near.

৩৶৵

They'd done just as Declan had suggested. The food. The wine. And oh, the glorious sex had been magnificent, he thought, as he watched her sleep, her hair splayed out over the pillow.

Even in the pale moonlight that filled the room, he could see the purple markings around her eye, and it made him angry. She seemed to have written it off as if it happened all the time, and maybe it did. He didn't know that side of her life. How many times was she threatened or hurt?

A part of him wanted to protect her forever, and another part was sure he'd cause her as much pain as being punched—if not more.

But he was comfortable being back home in the town he'd grown up in. It seemed normal. Even in the dark he chuckled to himself because he'd realized he'd slept in a different bed nearly every night he'd been there. This was by far the best one.

He couldn't help but reach out to touch her. Though he hadn't wanted to disturb her, she stirred.

"What's wrong?" Her voice was full of sex and sleep.

"Nothing. I was watching you, so I had to touch you."

"I'm going to be worthless in the morning, Declan. I need sleep."

"We can sleep in."

Her eyes opened wider. "I have to go to work. I have a maniac on the streets that I need to stop."

It hadn't crossed his mind that she'd work until the case was solved. And after that case, there would be another, and another. Sure, the same went for him, but weekends existed in his world. Lazy Saturday mornings with beautiful women, they happened— but obviously not today.

"Go back to sleep then. I didn't mean to wake you," he apologized, but she rolled over and onto him, straddling him. His body was wide awake, and reacted to her naked body towering over him.

"I'm awake now," she said as she took him inside of her and rode the glorious wave of sleepy morning sex until he watched her shudder in pleasure before he joined her.

THE STATION WAS QUIETER ON SATURDAY MORNINGS, BUT STILL, by the time she got there, the bustling had started. Lacy had opted to not wear sunglasses to work, and all eyes were on her. No doubt everyone there knew what had happened. It had happened to all of them, so not much was said.

"Morning," Carl spun in her direction from his office chair. "Have a good night?"

She set her overpriced cup of coffee on the desk and pulled off her jacket. "Sure. You?"

"Yeah, it was nice. Wife made dinner. We talked about my day, her day. Then she opted for a movie night at home. So we made popcorn and..."

"God, are you going to bore me to death at seven-thirty in the morning?"

"No. No, it gets better."

She wasn't sure about that. Lacy sat down in her chair and

picked up her coffee as Carl stood and walked toward her desk, sitting down on the edge.

"Fine. Continue."

"Where was I? Oh, yeah, we sat on the couch to watch a movie. I'm thinking Deadpool, right? She starts some Disney thing. I think we're watching Dumbo, it's when Dumbo is a baby or something. Then I realize it's a whole montage of Disney movies, but only the parts where there are babies."

Lacy lifted her eyes to watch him tell this story as she gripped her cup a little tighter.

"I'm bored out of my brain, mindlessly eating popcorn when I realize she's not watching this thing she's making me watch at all. So I finally turn to her and she's crying."

Lacy narrowed her stare on him. "You're an ass, aren't you? Holy shit! She's pregnant isn't she?"

His shoulders dropped. "You sure know how to ruin the ending of a good story."

Lacy sat her cup on the desk, jumped from her chair, and wrapped Carl in a tight embrace. "God, I was bored to death too. I was hoping it was going to end well."

He laughed against her. "Can you believe it? I'm going to be a dad."

Lacy pulled back. "You'll be the best one around, too. God, I can't believe it."

"Neither can I. In fact, I think I'm a little dizzy now," he joked as he sat in the chair in front of her desk.

Lacy pushed her coffee toward him. "You're in shock, still. I've seen this look."

He raised a brow. "On who?"

"People. Drink. Just because you knocked your wife up, we still have work to do."

He laughed as he sipped the coffee she'd offered. "Ah, Lacy, you can always bring me right back to earth."

"I try." She sat down at her desk and started up her computer.

She opened the email Amy Cartwright had sent her yesterday with her husband's car tracker and his log in information for his job.

She studied the log from his car as Carl walked behind her to look as well. "The trail is east of their house. He seems to only travel west."

"What's this location that he travels to nearly every day?" She pointed to the screen.

"Isn't that the church? Burton's church?"

"Cartwright goes to church every day?" she asked looking up at him. "Ten-fifteen?"

"Check against his log for work."

Lacy typed in the information Amy had given them and they verified that Cartwright clocked out at ten o'clock every day and back in at eleven-fifteen.

"It still doesn't put him anywhere near the murders."

"You're right. Has Autumn's family claimed her body yet?"

Carl walked over to his desk and looked at his own computer screen. "Yes."

"When is her funeral?"

He typed something into the computer. "Nothing is listed yet. Why?"

"I just wondered. It would be interesting to know if Amy Cartwright knew Autumn Taylor. She was at the funeral of Stacy and Carley Francess-Hastings."

Carl shrugged. "They all are about the same age. Maybe they knew each other. It's not a huge area."

"Big enough." She picked up a pen and tapped it to her chin. "I've been thinking that we're looking for a man."

"You're thinking that's wrong?"

"I don't know. I think we should consider that maybe one of Vaughn's other girlfriends might have been the jealous one. What if Amy Cartwright, for example, was afraid the others would tell her husband? What if she was so in love with Vaughn that she wanted him for herself?"

"Wasn't Burton's wife on Vaughn's list?"

Lacy nodded. "I think we should pay Pastor Ralph and his wife a visit. She wasn't at Stacy's funeral. He'd mentioned that she was sick when I spoke to him at the viewing."

"Does Cartwright visit the church on the weekends?"

She looked at the log. "Not on Saturdays."

"And she didn't mention her husband's visits to the church every day?"

"No."

"So let's assume she doesn't know about them. Let's check her work schedule and see how they line up."

Lacy nodded as she and Carl went to work looking up as much information as they could find online.

❧ 20 ❧

Declan had set up a makeshift office at his parents' kitchen table. Angie had promised to Skype him at ten o'clock to fill him in on the cases he'd been working on before he'd left.

Most of the cases he worked on never went to court. Such was the case the past week. Two of his cases had been passed to other lawyers, and he was okay with that. For the first time in his entire career, he wanted an empty schedule. He didn't want to have to worry about anything in New York as long as he was sitting in his parents' home.

As he picked up the mug of coffee, he looked at the email which Angie had forwarded to him as well. She thought he'd rather have it in writing. He'd read it four times so far, and it only made him happier with each read.

His ex-wife had seemed to have a change of heart, in light of his sister's murder. She pulled the suit she'd filed against him, no longer looking for a bigger share of his assets.

Of course, he'd have paid her anything if it meant his sister were still alive.

The mug in his hand began to shake, so he set it down and clasped his hands together. He could feel that breaking point coming, and he wondered when it would have him curled up in his bed in the dark, as it had with his mother. It reminded him, that he wanted to stop by Tom's and check on him. He also wanted him to bring the kids by. He thought it might help his parents to have them near, to get back to normal life as they'd known it a week ago.

Declan closed his laptop and pressed his folded hands to his forehead, his elbows rested on the table. Last night had offered him a great release of stress, and waking in Lacy's arms had been great comfort. But now he found he was missing her desperately, and he wondered when he'd ever been so desperate for someone's attention. He couldn't help but wonder if she'd be open to him staying with her again. Not for the sex, but the comfort of having her around. He hadn't realized he'd missed having someone in his space, in his arms.

Declan had thrived on his single life since his divorce. Hell, it was that need to be left alone that drove his wife away. So why would it be any different with Lacy? She was a strong-willed woman. At what point would she be tired of having him around?

Maybe he'd wait a few days before he showed up on her doorstep. He didn't want her to think he was needy, even if he was feeling that way. After all, she was working a case—a very important case. He'd been in her way since he arrived. Yeah, he'd give her some space to do her job.

❧

LACY PULLED UP ON THE SIDE OF THE CHURCH, CLOSEST TO THE parsonage where Pastor Ralph and his wife lived. Both of their cars were parked out back, new flowers had been planted in the pots by the door, and she watched as Pastor Ralph opened the front door, bent to pick up the newspaper, and saw them parked there.

He set the newspaper inside the front door and headed toward them as they climbed from the car.

"Good morning, Lacy and Carl. How are you this fine morning?" he asked.

"I'm doing great," Carl said quickly. "Found out I'm going to be a father."

"That's wonderful news," Pastor Ralph extended his hand to Carl who shook it. He then shifted his glance to Lacy. "And your father? Have you spoken to him? How is his fishing trip?"

"He's still out of range. I haven't spoken to him."

"I'm sure he's having a fantastic time. Can I interest either of you in some coffee and donuts? The lovely ladies of the choir were here this morning, practicing, and they left their goodies. I'm happy to share the wealth."

Carl nodded. "I could go for that."

Pastor Ralph headed toward the side door of the church, and they followed him inside and down stairs to the reception area where a box of donuts and a carafe of coffee sat near an old upright piano.

"Lacy, do you still play piano?" Pastor Ralph asked.

"It's been a very long time," she admitted.

Carl took a bite of a chocolate glazed donut he'd already pulled from the box. "You play?" he asked with his mouth full and chocolate stuck to his lips.

Pastor Ralph poured himself a cup of coffee. "Back when she was a little girl, my wife was her teacher. That was before we moved here."

Lacy turned toward them. "How is your wife? Is she feeling better?"

Pastor Ralph shrugged. "She decided to visit her sister. Her sister is into essential oils. She thought that would help her get better," he said. "I think it's all silliness, but who am I to keep sisters apart?"

"I thought I saw her car."

He nodded. "You did. Her sister came for her last night." Taking a bite of a sprinkle donut, he shifted a glance between them. "So what brought you two by? And Lacy, take your sunglasses off. It's dark down here."

She did as he said, and then watched as he set his donut down and moved to her. "Oh, sweetheart. What happened to you?"

"I had a run in with a suspect. It happens. It's no big deal."

"Yes it is," he said as he lifted his hand to her cheek. "How could anyone hurt such a sweet girl."

"Not everyone shares your opinion, sir."

He rested his hand on her shoulder. "They should. If they knew you like I do, no one would hurt you."

She smiled at the man who had been a big part of her life, and her father's. He'd helped get them on their feet when they'd moved to town, and was the driving force in counseling her father so that he'd be present for Lacy. She'd often wondered if she'd bought into the counseling a little more if she'd have been more rounded as a person. Lacy had rebelled. Sex and alcohol took the pain out of her mother's death. Looking back on it, the rebellious time was short, and it had landed her in the back seat of Declan's car—and then others. That brought a quick jolt to her heart. It had also set her in motion to do the job she now did so well. There had been a moment her senior year when she'd met a young girl whose mother had been killed by her father. In one moment that girl had lost both parents. Lacy had always been grateful that she'd had her father. But it had ignited the need to protect and serve. Right after high school she'd gone into the academy, and from there she'd climbed to detective. Her objective remained. She wanted to make sure no child was left behind by crimes, such as she was, and if and when they were, she wanted to make sure the criminal behind it was locked away.

The thought brought her back to the reason they'd paid Pastor Ralph a visit in the first place.

"I'm sorry we just dropped by unannounced, but I wanted to ask you about Sean Cartwright."

Pastor Ralph picked up his cup of coffee and sipped. "What about Sean? He's not in any trouble, is he?"

"We're just tying up loose ends. Has Cartwright been here every day for the past few weeks?"

"I've seen him."

"What was he doing here?"

Pastor Ralph set his coffee down on the table and clasped his hands in front of him. "Now, Lacy, you know that if someone came to me for any reason, I can't discuss that."

That gave her a lot of information right there. "Confidentiality."

"Right."

"We appreciate your time."

"You're going to leave, just like that?" Pastor Ralph smiled.

"I'd wanted to say hello to your wife, but will you pass on my well wishes to her?"

"Of course." He turned back to Carl and shook his hand again. "And congratulations on the baby."

"Thanks," Carl said as he lifted another donut from the box.

"And, Lacy, you should visit more often. Come to service. Come to visit. I miss our talks." He paused and looked at her, a smile settling on his lips. "You sure do look like your mother."

"My dad reminds me all the time."

They said their goodbyes and headed back to the car. As she backed out of the parking space, Pastor Ralph waved before he walked back into his house.

"He's a nice guy," Carl said, biting into the donut he'd taken with him.

"Uh-huh," she murmured as she pulled out onto the road.

"You have reservations?"

"I don't buy into religion. Yes, the man helped us out in a tight spot, but the Bible didn't fix my life. It didn't fix my father's either."

He took another bite. "What about Olivia Burton? You want to question her since she's involved with Vaughn?"

"Yeah. She's on the list of possible victims if we're holding onto the thought that someone is hurting those who are involved with Vaughn Price."

"So we call her at her sister's house?"

"That's my plan."

"What makes a pastor's wife have an affair?"

Lacy turned and gave him a look as she pulled up to a red light. "This one I understand. I know the woman, and she's a free thinker. She's muted by her husband quite a bit. But it's the life she chose, so in that case she should have left her husband if she no longer bought into it. However, when you have a voice and you have to take a backseat to your husband's beliefs, I believe you'd want something for yourself."

She moved through the light when it turned green and Carl finished his donut. "So Vaughn gives her a little freedom?"

"That's how I see it."

"As a woman, do you think he's a catch?"

She laughed as she pulled into the parking lot of the station and into a parking space as far from the door as she could find. "He's attractive, but not my type."

"You're into lawyers?" he teased as he opened the car door and stepped out of the car.

Lacy pulled the keys from the ignition and stepped out. "Don't go there, Moss."

"Hey, I noticed your mood was better today, that's all."

"Leave it at that, then."

"Oh, I don't think I can. I want details."

"What are you, some girl?"

"Sure. I'm a gossip girl, so how's the sex?"

On any other day she might have punched him in the arm and walked on, but today she found herself laughing. She stopped as Carl triggered the automatic door to the building to open. "Freaking fantastic," she said and walked through as Carl laughed.

It had been a long night, Declan thought, as he rubbed his eyes and poured himself a cup of coffee. He hadn't reached out to Lacy, and she hadn't sought him out either. That was all the proof he needed to back off a bit. Besides, somewhere between the time he left her bed and the time he crawled into his, he'd promised to take his niece and nephew to the mall and make a Build-A-Bear. What the hell had he been thinking?

When he arrived at Tom's house to pick up the kids they were running around the furniture, but Tom didn't seem to be about. Toby had let him in, and they'd both clung to him as if he were a waking tree. He'd promised them that if they brushed their teeth, and put on some clean clothes, they'd head to the mall. The fact that they were both still in their pajamas said things were definitely amiss.

He found Tom in his office, and he didn't look much better than the kids had.

"Everything okay?" Declan stood in the doorway and waited for Tom to answer, but when he didn't, he stepped in. "What's up. Are you okay?"

When he lifted his eyes, Declan saw that they were rimmed

red from crying, but there was anger in them. Tom's lips pursed as he held a letter in his hand. "I thought this was some kind of joke," he growled. "Just someone's sick joke. But now I don't know what to think of it."

Declan shut the door behind him. "What are you talking about?"

Tom shoved the letter at him. "I got this."

Declan looked over the letter and back up at Tom. "Oh, Tom. I'm so sorry." He sat down in the chair in the corner and read over the letter again, which detailed the affair his sister had had with Vaughn. "Who would have sent this to you?"

"Someone who knew," he said as he tossed the picture they'd sent with the letter. "That's them. They're goddamned kissing!"

Tom fisted his hands in hair.

"This is just shitty to send this to you."

"What's shitty is that my wife did that. I thought it was a big joke. She denied it when I asked her about it before. But, well, there's proof," he said pointing to the letter.

"So you already suspected it?"

"No. There was another damn letter the week before she died."

Declan's mouth went dry. "What letter?"

"I shredded the stupid thing when she denied it. I mean, my wife wouldn't lie to me."

"What did it say?"

"Something about the fact that she'd been having an affair and this person knew about it. It said they'd followed her and they'd prove she was what she was—a whore. It said she'd pay for what she'd done."

"And you shredded it? Didn't you take that seriously? Didn't you want to take it to the police?"

The tears rolled down Tom's cheeks. "Sean Cartwright got one too. And it didn't have Stacy's name in it. It just said *your wife*. I assumed if she denied it and Sean got one too, it was a fraud. Someone looking for something—money maybe. You know like those emails you get from princes in other countries wanting to give you their fortune." He wiped his eyes. "I had no idea."

"Listen to me. Don't change how you felt about my sister. She loved you more than anything, and you know that. She doted on those kids. They were her life."

"It's hard to keep that in mind now."

"Then go look at those photos that adorn your hallway, your mantel, your night stand. Even if she did have an affair, it didn't mean anything to her or she would have left. She didn't leave."

It hurt to argue for his sister when he'd given Vaughn a black eye over the whole thing because he was so pissed about it. But she did love Tom, that wasn't stretching the truth.

"It's going to take some time."

"Of course it is. Tom, don't forget her in your anger. Get some help. The kids need you."

He nodded. "You're taking them for the afternoon?"

"Yeah, but I don't want to leave you alone."

Tom chuckled. "I'm not suicidal. I'm not going to hurt anyone or anything. Though, if I see Vaughn Price..."

"You'll punch him in the face?"

"Yeah."

"If it's any consolation, I found out what had happened last night, and he's sporting a shiny black eye."

Tom's eyes widened. "You punched him?"

"They took him in for questioning. He asked for a lawyer. Couldn't help myself."

Tom nodded. "Good for you. Do they think he did this?"

"He's got solid alibis for all the murders. But they do think someone is going after the women he'd been with."

The tears were back in Tom's eyes. "And that included Stacy."

"I'm going to help Lacy get whoever did this. I'm going to take this letter to her and this will help."

"Catch the son-of-a-bitch. I need closure on this, Declan. I need to know this won't keep going. My kids need to move on."

"I'll do what I can. I'm not going back to New York until everything here is situated and whoever did this is behind bars."

Tom shook his head. "You can't give up your life for us. You have a job, a place."

"And that's all I have. My family needs me, and I'm finding out I need this place, too. Don't think about it as me giving up anything. I'm gaining some perspective."

The door to the office crept open and two young faces looked at them. Andi moved to her father's lap and climbed up, and Toby stepped into the office.

Tom pressed a kiss to Andi's head. "What are you two doing?"

"We want you to take us to build bears, Daddy," she said playing with the tie on her dress.

"Uncle Declan was going to take you."

She looked at Declan with a look of apology, but it was clear they wanted their father.

"Why don't you take them. Get out of the house. Let me take this to Lacy. Come to Mom and Dad's for dinner tonight. It's time to make a new normal."

Tom nodded. "Okay. Let me know what she says about it."

"Will do."

Declan drove by the police station after he left Tom and the kids. A quick sweep of the parking lot told him Lacy wasn't there. He drove to her house next and was pleased to find her car parked outside. The letter in his pocket, which Tom had given him, was making him itchy. The person who had ended his sister's life had touched that letter, written it, determined when they'd send it to Tom. Everything about it made his blood boil, and he found himself getting angrier by the moment as if the hate in the letter seeped into his skin. How was it that more than one man had these kinds of letters, but no one turned them over? Had the world become so cynical that they didn't even believe threats anymore?

He parked his car and walked up to the front door. He rang the doorbell and waited, but Lacy didn't answer. He rang again, and then thought he could hear the faint sound of someone grunting from around the back of the house.

Panic set into his chest as he began to run toward the sound. Grunting, punching, kicking. They were all distinct sounds of a scuffle, and his heart raced in his chest as he neared the garage which was detached from the house.

When he reached the door, he found that it was already open as he burst through, nearly falling over the threshold and having to teeter to balance himself. Lacy let out a scream just as she stopped the swinging of the heavy bag she'd obviously just been kicking, by the stance she had taken.

"Declan, what the hell are you doing?" she yelled as she pulled her headphones from her ears.

"Do you have any idea how loud you are from outside?" he asked, noticing that all the windows to the garage were open. He looked around and realized there was no way she'd ever parked a car in there. The place was a well set up gym.

"I'm loud?"

"I thought you were in trouble," he argued. "Don't bust my ass. I have a break in your damn case and you need me."

She pulled the band from her arm that held her phone and laid it, and the headphones, on an old workbench. "I need the evidence."

That stung, but he figured he deserved it. He was being snippy with her, and there had been no reason for it.

Declan pulled the letter from his pocket and handed it to her. As she took it, she looked up into his eyes, but he couldn't get a reading. Was she mad because he hadn't called her all day? Was she thinking he should move in for a kiss? Or was she as pissed at him as she looked for busting in on her workout?

"Tom got this?"

He nodded. "Yes. It's the second one."

Her eyes lit with anger. "Second? What the hell? Why didn't he tell me that?"

"It came before Stacy was killed. He said it seemed generic, and she denied it. He trusted her. It helped that Sean Cartwright got one too."

"Son-of-a-bitch. He didn't report it either?"

Declan shook his head. "Tom said it was written very generically. But go to Sean. Tom shredded the other one. But this is a low thing to send someone two days after you bury your wife."

"It was pretty low to kill them, too."

He scowled, but her eyes remained angry and focused on him.

Lacy picked up her phone and earbuds, then walked past him and right out the door.

He followed, jogging to catch up with her. "You mad?"

"Would it matter?"

He reached for her arm to slow her stride, but she came toward him, and he was fairly sure she just might finish her workout by punching him. Declan took a step back and raised his hands in surrender.

"I get it. You're upset."

"I am. And that pisses me off. And do you know why I'm upset?"

"Fill me in, please."

She set her jaw, narrowed her eyes on him, and then turned and walked into the back door of the house.

Assuming she was still wanting to argue, he followed.

LACY STORMED INTO THE KITCHEN AND RIPPED OFF THE fingerless gloves she had on. She brushed the back of her hand over her lip to wipe away the sweat. She'd worked herself into a tizzy over Declan, and it made her mad as hell. Then having him show up with information on the case, well that just made her angrier.

She focused on opening the fridge and pulling out a bottle of water. Opening it, she drank down most of it standing there with the door open, fully aware that he was watching her.

When she turned around, she saw him leaning a hip against the counter, his arms folded in front of him casually, as if he belonged in the stupid kitchen.

"Why do you look so smug?" she asked sipping from the bottle again.

"You're sexy when you're mad."

Oh, and didn't that just make her madder? "Well then I must be looking like a freaking Victoria's Secret model right now."

"Very close."

"You're a pig. Why don't you go now?"

"Why don't you tell me why you're so upset. This isn't all about the letter."

It would be easier to kick his ass out of her house. To watch him walk away without the honor of knowing just why she was stewing, that would be fine with her—but it wasn't fine.

The fact that she wanted to tell him why she was upset, that didn't even make sense to her. She'd never cared enough about a man to tell him anything. So why now? Why him?

"I don't need a man in my life," she laid it out matter-of-factly.

"Okay."

"I don't want to have to think about where you are or what you're doing."

"Good."

"Stop that." She felt her muscles tighten. "You're trying to aggravate me."

"I think I already did that. Is this because I didn't call you last night or come over? Because I thought long and hard over that and I don't want to be in trouble for my decisions."

"No see, that's why I'm pissed off. I don't want to give a crap whether you called me or came over. I don't want to think that just because we had sex it enables you to think one way or another."

"But you're not buying that, are you?"

"No," she blurted out the word so fast she wasn't sure it was her voice that she'd heard say it. "Damnit, Matthews, I have a job to do."

"And you're damn good at it."

"I am. I don't want this messing it up."

"And did I mess up anything today? I'm trying to figure this out, too, you know. I don't just want sex from you. I want something more."

Her eyes were fixed on him. She wasn't even sure she could blink. "What does that mean?"

"I don't know. All I know is I want to be with you. Right now my world has been turned inside out and you're here." He raked his fingers through his hair. "Let's get it out there, the sex was phenomenal. If it was the last sex I ever had, I'd die happy."

She felt the small tug on the corner of her mouth, but she fought it.

Declan took a step toward her and then stopped. "Lacy, all I know is I didn't want to get in your way. So I didn't call. I didn't come over. I'm not a needy man, but I'm afraid I could be when it comes to you."

"Why?"

"Because I feel my need for you taking over, and I do want to be with you. I don't want to make you push me away because I'm in the way."

Lacy pursed her lips and nodded. "That's why I'm pissed, Matthews. I don't want to depend on you coming around. Any other man in the world I wouldn't even care. But I found out today that I cared, and that's what's got me all worked up."

Now he moved to her until he could reach for her hands. "We suck at this."

She chuckled. "We do. But you're right. The sex was phenomenal."

"Maybe it would fix this awkward stage we're in right now."

"What? More sex?"

He nodded as he moved in closer to her. "I mean it's worth a try."

"I have to call Moss and follow up on this lead."

She watched the darkness in his eyes ease. "Right."

"But, I can't go into work sweaty and a mess. I need a shower, and I sure could use someone to wash my back."

The darkness clouded his eyes again, right before he scooped her up in his arms and carried her off toward the bathroom.

ジ 2 2 ジ

L acy's step was quick as she walked from her car and into the station. Carl's car was already there, and she was feeling guilty for pulling him away from his wife. He'd made it clear they were cleaning out the spare room for the nursery. Though when he said it on the phone, she wasn't sure if it was anger or thankfulness that had filled his voice.

She jogged up the stairs and flung open the door to head toward her desk. The faces of those sitting at their desks was never good on a Sunday. But crime happened always. It didn't care if everyone wanted a weekend off.

Lacy slowed her pace when she noticed Carl wasn't sitting at his desk alone. When they noticed her walking toward them, both sets of eyes watched her. How did he have Sean Cartwright sitting there already?

"Sean. Carl." She gave them each a nod. "How are we today?"

"She wants to paint the room green, Lacy. I'm old fashioned. I want it blue with a big ole Dodgers decal on the wall," Carl complained and she found that she chuckled.

"It'll be a girl then."

"I have no complaints on pink with a Disney princess." He

exchanged looks with Sean. "Sean has something for us that might be of interest to you. He called me today and asked to come in."

She looked at Sean who pulled an envelope from his pocket.

"This came today, and Amy doesn't know about it. In fact, she doesn't know that I know she's had an affair with Vaughn Price."

Lacy nearly wanted to sigh as she reached for the letter and sat back on her desk. "It's the same," she said to Carl.

Sean cleared his throat. "I know that Tom Watts got a previous letter too. Under protest, I tore the other one up."

"Under protest to who? Who told you to do that?"

Sean folded his hands in his lap, and lowered his head a moment before looking up at her. "I've been going to counseling since I found out about the affair. Every day I spend an hour with Pastor Ralph Burton. I don't want to lose my wife over this," he assured them.

He wiped his hands on his pant legs as he took a deep breath. "Amy and I were each other's firsts and we stayed celibate until we were married. She had a moment where her judgement lapsed, and seriously I think she was needing to sow her oats, if you will. She confronted me that she thought I'd been having an affair. I wasn't. I don't know where she got it in her head, but I wasn't. I assume that's why she started this thing with Vaughn. But I love her. I want her to work through this. I know she hasn't seen him in a while. Vaughn that is."

Carl leaned back in his seat and crossed his arms in front of him. "So you've known, but she doesn't know you know."

"Correct."

"And Pastor Ralph is working you though this?"

Sean nodded. "He's a fine Christian. He thinks that I'm doing right by my marriage."

Lacy set the letter down on her desk. "Three of the women Vaughn Price has had affairs with have turned up dead. Tom Watts got two letters as well, and his wife is gone. Aren't you fearful for Amy?"

"That's why I'm here. Counseling can save my marriage, but if this guy isn't caught, it might not save my wife."

He had a solid head on him, Lacy thought. "Does Pastor Ralph have any thoughts on the murders? Have you discussed it?"

He shook his head. "Not really. We just pray—a lot. And we read the Bible," he admitted, though Lacy knew that was part of the counseling deal. "She'll come around and she'll admit to her sin."

Lacy had heard these words before, she thought. Her own father prayed until he just couldn't do it anymore. After her mother's murder, he fell into a dark place. Even now, nearly twenty years later, he'd slide into the darkness. He'd learned to cope. Pastor Ralph had given him the tools to come back from it.

"If you get any more of these letters, or there is any correspondence, please contact us," she said.

"I will," Sean agreed. "But I'd like to ask that if you speak to Amy, don't tell her I know. I'll keep her safe. I just don't want her to know that I know about her affair. I want her to come to me."

"Not a problem."

Sean stood and shook each of their hands before walking out of the squad room.

They both watched him leave, and then exchanged looks. Carl shook his head before he rose and walked to Lacy's desk. "What the hell is wrong with the world? Women having affairs. Men waiting for the woman to confess."

"Affairs are normal," she said as she compared the letters that Sean and Tom had surrendered. "People are curious."

"Well that's why they should satisfy that curiosity before they're married. I know for a fact I won't have this problem in my marriage. Both Heather and I have pasts. We recognize that and we were satisfied."

"Satisfied?"

"I mean, we don't have to experience other people again. We

have each other and it's enough." He narrowed his eyes on her. "And I mean that as a positive thing."

"I'll take your word for it," she said looking down at the letters. "These are exactly the same. But I take it Sean didn't get a photo?"

Carl shrugged. "He didn't mention it."

"This makes me wonder, does Pastor Ralph have one of these letters too?"

Carl's eyes grew wide. "If he got one, I wonder if he'd ignore it too? And we have to consider that he's seen one of these letters, if not multiple ones, so would he assume that they were just someone trying to egg on men?"

"What if he got a picture?"

Carl considered. "I suppose that would give him something to seriously question."

"I'm going to find Olivia Burton's sister's phone number and give her a call. We need to talk to her. Her life is in danger too. Someone seems to know all the women Vaughn was having an affair with."

"I'm going to run down to the convenience store and get myself a Coke. I might buy a few to stock up—for myself."

She looked up at him and chuckled.

He walked to his desk and pulled on his jacket. "Can I get you anything?"

"You're offering to buy me a Coke?"

"God, Pratt, how does Declan put up with you? You're truly a pain in the ass. I'll bring you a Coke and a Snickers. It'll be the perfect dinner for you."

She watched him walk toward the elevator and disappear behind its doors. He was right. She was a pain in the ass, but usually it wasn't a problem. No one ever had to care, but it seemed as though Declan did.

WHILE LACY WAITED FOR HER SNICKERS DINNER TO ARRIVE, she found Olivia Burton's sister's information. She'd placed a call to her home and to her cell phone, but neither one was answered. Stella O'Neal was a nurse at an assisted living facility, so Lacy placed a call there as well. It too was a dead end. She wasn't working on Sunday, but she left a message and hoped that Stella would call back, or Olivia for that matter. And because she was feeling uneasy about it all, she connected with the local police station near Stella O'Neal's house. There had been no reports of missing persons, and no suspicious activity.

Carl walked back through the squad room, a Coke in each hand. "You look like you could use this," he said setting one of them on Lacy's desk. "What's wrong?"

"Stella O'Neal, Olivia Burton's sister, isn't answering any of the phone numbers that come up for her. She's not at work today either."

"Nice day out. Maybe they went sightseeing or something."

"That's what I want to think. But my gut isn't buying it."

"You think someone got to Olivia Burton?"

She shrugged. "No one has said that she or her sister are missing, so I'm probably just getting antsy. I want this done, Moss. We're going on a week with very few leads."

Just as she pulled the top to her Coke, and had the satisfaction of hearing it fizz, Vaughn Price stepped out of the elevator and walked straight to them.

His face was red as if he'd run to the station.

"Vaughn, what's up?" Lacy stood and moved to him. "You don't look good."

"Fire. Someone set fire to a bush outside my house."

"You're sure someone set it?"

He nodded and tried to catch his breath. "It was just the one bush. But this was taped to my door when I went out to put the fire out."

He handed her a piece of paper and she sucked in a breath

when she saw what was on it. It was no wonder Vaughn looked so bad. There were pictures of Carley Francess-Hastings, Stacy Watts, and Autumn Taylor, all dead as if the person who killed them took a souvenir photo of each. Then at the bottom of the letter was a photo of Amy Cartwright getting into her car outside her house.

"It's a warning," Lacy said as she handed the letter to Carl. "He's stalking Amy Cartwright."

"I'll call her in. We'll get her under protection," Carl said moving to his desk.

Lacy pulled Vaughn to the chair in front of her desk and handed him the open Coke. "Drink this. You're in shock."

He did as she said. "Lacy, I didn't want this to happen to anyone. I had no idea it would. I was just—God, I was just having fun."

"Someone doesn't like your fun."

"But who has it out for me? You've talked to all their husbands."

She nodded. "We can't find Olivia Burton," she told him and his face grew pale. "Drink that Coke," she ordered.

"What about Crystal?"

"We'll put some protection on her too, but it doesn't seem as though the unattached women you've been with are a problem. Just the married ones."

"Don't let him get to the others. Lacy, I'm sick. I really did love them all. I'm not some sex-crazed guy."

"I know." Or at least she thought she did. "We're going to get to the bottom of this. I don't want anyone else to die on my watch, but they're trying to spook everyone now."

"What does that mean?"

"Everyone got some kind of a letter. I'd expect some angry husbands to be waiting for you too."

Vaughn's eyes widened. "They know?"

She nodded. "You might think about asking for a transfer at

work. A new city might be a good idea when this is all done. Until then, you don't leave this building."

He wiped his hands over his face. "I can't believe this is because of me."

"So other than spiteful husbands, who else have you pissed off?"

He shrugged. "God, Lace, who haven't I pissed off? I have a quick temper. I've fired a few people in the past few years. Even my own mother gets mad when I call, because I don't do it often enough."

"Okay, I want a list of the people you've fired. Let's just get a feel on everyone." She narrowed her gaze on him. "By the way, that black eye you have, did you walk into a door?"

His lips tightened. "Yeah, something like that."

Lacy grinned as she sat down behind her desk and began a search on social media for Olivia Burton. But she couldn't have been more proud of Declan at that moment. A bit of her wanted to punch Vaughn Price in the face too.

❧ 23 ❧

Declan sat on the front steps of Lacy's house, a bouquet of grocery store flowers resting on his lap and a bag of food from his mother next to him on the step.

It was nearly eight o'clock, and he couldn't imagine she'd be at the station much longer, but as he'd been sitting there for nearly forty-five minutes, he now wasn't so sure.

When he'd decided to call her, and lose the element of surprise, he saw the headlights starting down the street. Luckily it was her car, and she slowed in front of the house.

He could already see the steely-eyed look she was giving him as she parked and climbed from the car.

Resting her arms on the top of the car, she looked up at him. "What are you doing on my steps?"

"Waiting for you. We had a family dinner at my parents' house, but you were working. So my mom sent leftovers for you."

She drummed her fingers on the roof of the car. "What did she send?"

"Get up here and find out."

Lacy hesitated for a moment before closing the car door and walking toward him. "Did she send flowers too?"

"Nope, that's all me. I get credit for being sappy."

"Flowers die, Matthews."

"They sure do. But for a while they give off joy. I thought you could use some joy," he said, noticing that her face twitched as if she wanted to smile, but it would have been out of character for her.

Picking the bag up from the step, she moved to the door and pushed it open.

"You don't lock your door?" He wasn't sure if that was a scolding or sheer amazement for what he considered stupidity.

"Sucks that you've been sitting out here this whole time when you could have been inside where it's nice and I have a wide selection of TV channels."

Declan couldn't help but laugh at that.

Lacy set the bag on the kitchen table and looked inside. "Is this pot roast and potatoes?"

"It is."

"Salad and a roll?"

"There were two rolls, but I got hungry sitting out there. Will I be expecting that in the future? You know, you getting called out on the weekend and being gone all day."

Lacy moved from the bag as if it were hot, paced the kitchen, then opened the refrigerator door. She looked inside for a moment, finally pulling out a bottle of water.

"You want one?" she snapped out the offer.

"I'd love one."

She pulled out another bottle and tossed it at him before slamming the door, opening her bottle, and drinking it down. When she paced again, Declan moved to her and held her by the shoulders.

"What's wrong?"

Lacy jerked away. "This isn't going to work. This is a mistake."

"Pot roast is never a mistake."

She looked at him for a moment as if he hadn't understood

what she was getting at—but he knew. He'd wait until she could thrash him with her words. It was what she needed to do. He'd been married. He knew the routine.

"You sit on my porch and wait for me? You bring me leftovers because I missed a family meal? And what the hell is that talk of *should I expect that in the future* shit? You don't have to expect anything in the future. I've lived like this for years and I'm very happy."

Declan nodded. "You look happy."

"You're an asshole."

"I have it in writing. You don't get divorced when you're not an asshole."

"I'll bet I'd get along just fine with your wife."

"Ex-wife. The ex part is particularly important since you and I have a thing."

He could see the red in her skin creep up her neck and into her face.

"We had sex."

"We did. I think we both agreed it was fantastic sex."

"That's not a relationship, Matthews."

Rubbing his chin, he fought back the grin that wanted to surface. "It is when you're really interested in someone."

"And you're interested in me?"

"I could have headed back to New York. I chose to stay."

"To help Tom and your parents."

"Yep, that too."

Lacy pressed her fingers to her eyes. "You're still an asshole. I don't like these games."

"And I don't like that you don't lock your door. Now, can we be civilized and sit down? Heat up your dinner. Let me stay. Maybe we could catch a ball game on one of those many TV channels you said you had."

"You're not staying the night."

"I think we should discuss that later—after you've had a decent meal."

LACY HADN'T THOUGHT MUCH ABOUT FOOD UNTIL SHE'D looked in the bag. Now she was hungry, and maybe that's why she was arguing with him. Or maybe it was why she hadn't kicked his ass out of her house. She just didn't have the strength for it.

He kept quiet while she heated up the pot roast and pulled out the butter for the potatoes and the roll. When it was warm, she sat back down at the table to eat.

"Did you get any further with the letters today?" he asked, but she was sure he was making small talk. There was no reason for her to think that he'd only stayed in town to meddle into their investigation.

"Vaughn got a letter too. Whoever we're looking for must have done a mass mailing." She took a bite of the roast and moaned. "This is good."

"My mom is an amazing cook."

She washed down the bite with a sip of water. "I want to talk to Olivia Burton soon though. Her life is in danger and she needs to know. Pastor Ralph said she was staying with her sister. He's yet to come to us with a letter, but he might not believe it if he gets one. However, I can't get a hold of Olivia's sister."

"So what do you do?"

"She's only forty minutes away. I think I'll drive up there tomorrow and pay her a visit."

"With Carl?"

"Carl is going to the doctor with his wife. They're having a baby."

"Lucky them," he said with a smile she didn't much care for. "Then I'll be ready to go with you when you leave."

"Police business, Matthews."

"Lawyer business, Pratt. Vaughn is still a suspect."

"And you're defending him?"

"I need another opportunity to punch him."

Lacy laughed. "He says he got hit by a door."

"Unlucky S.O.B."

DECLAN HELD HER AS SHE SLEPT, HIS FACE BURIED IN HER HAIR, her soft skin under his hands. Making love to her wasn't enough, he thought as he listened to her gentle breath. He was going with her to Olivia Burton's sister's house because he wanted to protect her. Of course, he'd never tell her that. In fact, he was quite sure when it came to push and shove, she'd be protecting him. But the longing for her went deeper than physical, and that had his heart making decisions.

Closing his eyes, he tried to wipe his mind clear so that he could rest. But his mind kept buzzing. He just couldn't figure out which angle they were missing. Why had this maniac killed three women and not left a trace? Now he was sending out letters?

Declan owed it to his niece and nephew to help find their mother's killer. He owed it to his sister. A churning in his gut made him open his eyes again. If in fact they found out it was Vaughn Price, he'd kill the man himself.

❧ 24 ❧

The grip Lacy had on the steering wheel told her she should have put up a fight when Declan climbed into the car that morning. She didn't need him going with her. She didn't need him in her business. And she certainly didn't need to be waking up in his arms the way she had that morning.

Gripping the wheel tighter, she wondered what woman in their right mind would get pissed off about a man holding her, kissing her neck, and whispering *Good morning* in her ear.

Lacy wasn't cut out for this relationship crap. Besides, it had only been a week. No matter what Declan said, he'd be heading back to New York soon. He'd already been on the phone most of the morning with his office. He had a life away from there, and he needed to get back to it. In another month, Lacy would just be a memory from home—again.

When they pulled up to the little cottage house that matched the address of Stella O'Neal, Lacy put the car in park. "I'll be out as soon as I can," she said as she opened the door.

"I'm not staying in the car."

"This is official police business, Declan. You have no business going in there."

A smile crept across his mouth. "We're making progress. You do know my first name."

Lacy let out a groan. "Stay here. There aren't going to be any problems."

She climbed from the car and headed to the front door. She hadn't really expected him to stay in the car, but he had, she noted, as she rang the doorbell.

A moment later the front door opened, and there stood Stella O'Neal—a woman who was the spitting image of her sister.

"Ms. O'Neal, I'm Detective Lacy Pratt," she said as she showed her badge to the woman.

"I got your message. I don't think I can offer you any information, Ms. Pratt," she said still holding the door protectively open only a few inches. "I haven't talked to my sister in years. I don't know where she is."

And that was the twist that Lacy hadn't expected. "Would you mind talking to me for a few moments anyway? Any information you might be able to give me would be of great assistance to my case."

"She's in trouble, isn't she?" Stella shook her head. "Nearly sixty-years-old, and she's still in trouble?" Stella opened the door. "You can come in for a few minutes. I don't really want to get involved. I hope you'll understand."

"I appreciate that, Ms. O'Neal."

"You can call me Stella."

She led Lacy to the living room and gestured with her hand for her to take a seat on the sofa. Stella sat in a well-worn chair across the room.

"Stella, I was under the impression that your sister was here staying with you because she was under the weather."

A slow fat cat walked into the room and studied Lacy before she jumped up into Stella's lap. Stella brushed a hand over her as she settled in. "This is Betsy. She's as old as dirt, but must like my company enough to stick around," she said before lifting her eyes to Lacy. "I'm sorry someone told you that. Olivia and I haven't spoken in nearly twenty years."

"I was unaware of that."

"Twins are supposed to be very close. We never were."

"Where was your sister when you did last see her?"

Stella considered her answer. "She was recently out of her second stint in rehab. Olivia has always had a problem with alcohol. She'd gotten involved with a minister of all things. I assume he was trying to save her soul."

"Are you speaking of Pastor Ralph Burton?"

Stella nodded. "I think that was his name. I've only met him a few times. I know that they moved, shortly after they were married, to a new town."

Lacy thought about the time line and how it matched up to her own life. When she'd met the Burtons, they were already married. However, as a teenager, she could have cared less as to how long they'd been married. All she knew was that her mother had deceived them before she was murdered, so with broken hearts they picked up their life and moved.

She shook her own troubles from her mind. "The reason I'm here is because Olivia might have had a run-in with a potential serial killer. We're trying to find her to protect her."

Stella's hand went to her chest. "Oh, dear." Her breath grew more rapid and Lacy moved to the edge of her seat.

"Are you alright?"

Stella nodded. "I knew some day something like this would happen. I don't care who you marry, if you're a bad seed, you're a bad seed."

"You think she might have gotten into some trouble?"

Stella lowered her hand. "Of course I think that. My sister seemed to lack all the common sense I was graced with." The cat readjusted on Stella's lap. "Detective, I would guess that she might be using this opportunity to run and start over. If the world thought she might have disappeared, then she wouldn't have to answer to anyone."

"The woman you're describing to me is much different than the one I know," Lacy admitted.

"Tell me, are you always the job? Is there a side to Detective Pratt that maybe no one else knows? We all have a side to us that we keep to ourselves. Olivia has a wild side. She might have walked the walk of a preacher's wife, but deep down inside there is a woman crying out for help in the worst possible way. I'm sure you'll find her drunk under some rock somewhere, but that's all I can tell you. I don't know where you might find her."

Lacy nodded, disappointed in the information. She'd truly hoped to find Olivia Burton sitting on her sister's couch.

She thanked Stella for her time. "If you do hear from your sister would you please let me know?" she asked as she handed her a business card. "I want to help her."

Stella took the card. "If I hear from her," she agreed.

Lacy walked out of the house and toward the car where Declan stood leaned up against it. He didn't say anything to her, but he scanned a look over her as if he were trying to read her.

She walked to the driver's side, opened the door, and slid in as he did the same. Lacy lowered her sunglasses from her head to her face, started the car, and pulled away from the curb.

"She's not there, huh?" he asked.

"I didn't say that."

"You didn't have to. I can read you. I'd venture to guess she hasn't seen her in a long time."

"What are you, some kind of mind reader?"

"I'm a lawyer. A good one," he reminded her, and she decided that was a skill for sure.

"Hasn't talked to her in nearly twenty years. Our beloved Olivia Burton has more than an extra marital affair going on. Her sister says she's been in and out of rehab for alcoholism. She seems to think that Pastor Ralph was saving her when he married her. It lines up about the time we moved here after my mother died. I didn't know they'd been recently married. I just knew my father seemed to find peace with Pastor Ralph's guidance, and he needed that."

Declan turned slightly in his seat and pulled off his sunglasses. As she slowed for a stop light she shifted a glance his direction. Those blue eyes seared right into her and sent a sizzle through her.

"What?"

"Pull over."

She looked around. "I'm in the middle of the intersection."

"Next light. Take a left into that parking lot."

Lacy set her jaw, and when the light turned she pulled through to the next light and did as he said. When she'd parked, she climbed from the car and skirted the front of it as he met her. "Ralph knew you and your father before you moved here."

"Yeah. I've told you that."

"Right. Did he know your mom too?"

"Yes." She raked her fingers through her hair. "Where are you going with this?"

Declan reached his hands to her arms and held them there. "You told me your mother had an affair."

She tried to shrug out of his grip. "I don't want to talk about that."

His hands remained firm. "Let's do. I know it hurts and I know you don't want to talk about it. I get that." He kept his eyes on hers. "Do you know who your mother had an affair with?"

"This isn't your business, Matthews."

"I'm making it my business."

The tears stung her eyes and her heart squeeze until it was nearly unbearable. "Yes. Does that make you happy? Yes, I know who it was."

"Who."

"Don't go there."

"Who?"

She pursed her lips hoping it would push back the tears. "One of my teachers. Okay? Are you very happy now? She was screwing one of my teachers. He had a wife and three kids who left him after that. Two weeks later my mother was murdered. A month after that, after he'd been interrogated to the brink of insanity, he committed suicide. He had a solid alibi for the night she was murdered, but it ate at him enough that he took his life. He left those three girls fatherless."

The tears broke the barrier she'd fought so hard to put up.

Declan pulled her to his chest and held her tightly. She sobbed like she hadn't sobbed in years. Her mother broke up more than one family and for what? Sex? It disgusted her—all of it did. She'd never be able to look at Vaughn the same way again, even though she knew in her heart he had nothing to do with the murders. As her breathing slowed, she took comfort in Declan's lips pressed to the top of her head. His arms wrapped protectively around her. She'd never have admitted, and she wouldn't now either, that she needed this—this kind of moment.

In one short week, she'd fallen in love with Declan Matthews all over again. How was she going to keep her life on track when he went home?

Lacy pulled back and wiped her eyes under the lenses of her sunglasses, which offered her some dignity. "I'm fine now. Let's go."

Declan placed his hands on her shoulders, giving them a gentle squeeze. "Not yet. I have a few more thoughts and they're just going to piss you off and set you right back into tears."

Perhaps it would be fair to punch him in the gut, she thought, and that even brought a small hint of humor into her heart which lightened her mood the slightest bit.

"Can it wait twenty minutes? If you're going to have me babbling like an idiot, let me do it on my own couch in a pair of sweat pants."

He smiled, and the dimple in his cheek winked, making her heart squeeze a bit tighter. "That's fine with me. First rule though, you can't kick me out no matter how mad you get at me."

"You're going to take me down some very dark road, huh?"

"I've worked my share of murder trials. I've defended the guilty and not guilty. I can read people. Let me work through a few scenarios with you and see if it gives us some new game plan."

"Gives me a new game plan. You're not part of this, Matthews."

He shook his head. "You've already forgotten my name."

She couldn't help but let the chuckle escape. "I'll listen. I'm irritated that I don't have someone in custody over this. There is someone out there who needs to pay for what they've done. I need to find them, and Olivia Burton. Her life is in danger."

"Let's go home and get comfy then."

He released her shoulders and turned back to climb into the car, but his words dangled in the air and had Lacy's head swimming. *Let's go home.* She could honestly say she'd never wanted a man to say something like that to her. It wasn't something she bought into. But hearing Declan say it so innocently made her crave it.

This had grown more complicated and she needed to focus on finding the man who murdered her friend and his sister. There wasn't time for daydreaming until someone was behind bars.

❧ 25 ❧

Declan poured a glass of wine for each of them and found enough food in the house to make a little tray with some cheese, crackers, fruit snacks in a little package, and even some beef jerky. It was nearing lunch time, he was going to make her dig deeper into her own past, and he figured if anyone deserved to drink in the middle of the day, it was her.

He set the plate on the coffee table as she emerged from the bedroom in her gray sweatpants with the word NAVY down the leg. She'd pulled on a fitted tank top, and his mind wandered away from the plate of food to think of how he knew what she looked like under that tank. Swallowing hard, he picked up her glass of wine and handed it to her.

"It's the middle of the day," she scolded, as he knew she would.

"Yep, and we're in your house and you're wearing sweatpants for comfort. I thought this would add to the comfort."

Lacy looked down at the plate. "What's that?"

"A horrible attempt at being a little fancy. You have no food."

"I don't eat at home very often."

"That should change. You should eat a better breakfast than a

piece of toast on your way out the door and fast food all day long."

Lacy looked down at her body. "Do I look unfit to you?"

"No. I'm just saying you deserve it."

"Great, then why don't you move in and cook for me if you're so worried."

Declan lifted his glass to his lips and smiled from behind it before taking a sip. He let the wine linger on his tongue a moment. "Sounds like you're making me an offer, Lace."

"And you still have a life, New York boy. So why don't we sit down and get this over with. I really don't want to think about what you're going to dive into."

Lacy sat down on the sofa and pulled her feet up under her. Declan sat on the other end of the sofa. Looking at her he thought he liked her offer, but he liked the busy atmosphere of the city too. Clark Gulch, Utah wasn't even close to New York, but in the past twenty years it had grown to nearly three-hundred thousand people from the one-hundred when he'd grown up there. Once a city with two high-schools, now they had four. Recreation centers had popped up and a whole slew of housing developments. Towns that used to be twenty minutes away without a stoplight in between them were now nearly joined.

With another sip of his wine he thought there just might be enough need for a lawyer of his caliber.

Lacy took a piece of cheese from the plate and popped it into her mouth. "Okay, let's get this over with. I don't like crying. I don't like thinking about what my mother did, and what my father and I went through. I'm pissed that there is a killer out there stalking his next victim. And I'm worried that if we don't find Olivia Burton soon, she'll *be* our next victim."

"Twenty minutes."

"That's all you've got. Go."

Declan sipped his wine and then set the glass on the table.

"How long did your mom have an affair before she was murdered?"

He watched as her jaw tightened. "Six months. She lied to us for six months."

"How much longer before you knew about it?"

She took another piece of cheese. "Maybe another six. I don't know," her tone edged with ice. "Maybe a little longer."

"Your dad went to Pastor Ralph for counseling?"

"Yes." She shook her head. "I mean not just then. They'd been going through a rough patch. I assume that's what led her down the path she took." She swallowed hard. "They found my mother's body nearly two weeks after she'd been missing. We were both crazy with worry and didn't quite know what to think. There was a part of me that assumed she'd run out on us."

She sipped at her wine. "Much like our victims, she'd been strangled. She wasn't abused or raped. My father did his duty to bury her and keep his head clear for me. A few weeks later depression set in and he started missing work." She took a breath. "The man he worked for was a good man. He told him to get some help and he'd hold his job for him."

"The world needs more people like that."

She agreed with a nod. "My dad sought out some counselor who told him he should share my mother's infidelity with me. By that time, he'd learned of the affair and the death of the man to suicide." She sipped her wine. "He told me about the affair later. I assume he thought if he waited until I was a little older I'd get it. I'd forgive her, but instead I turned against him. I turned against everyone. That's when he went to Pastor Ralph. I can't say he found God in that moment, but he figured it would help."

"Pastor Ralph helped you then?"

She laughed now. "Oh, he tried. God wasn't on my side. I was twelve and had lost my mother to the hands of some maniac. My father had turned to the Bible as if it held the answers to why my mother did what she did and why someone did what they did to her."

Trying to cure a teenager with the Bible had disaster written all over it, he thought. Well, if she wasn't into God, that was. It might have helped anyone else. "I don't think I realized that your father did that."

"You don't really know him. I don't blame you for not knowing what kind of man he is." She eased back against the sofa. "He's a good man. Perhaps not as church-going as he was once, but he's begun to find solace in nature."

"That's where he is now?"

"Yes. He's in Alaska fishing. That brings him more peace than his Bible."

"And his relationship with Pastor Ralph?"

She let out a long breath. "They still have one. He goes to church on Sunday if he's in town. But he's found his own peace, just like I said."

Declan reached his hand out to touch hers. "But Pastor Ralph was why you moved to Clark Gulch? That seems as if your father and Pastor Ralph had quite a relationship."

She shrugged, not much enjoying his questioning into her past. "Dad thought if it was good enough for a man of God, it was good enough for him. There was work here. It meant a new school for me. New friends. We'd lived outside Seattle when my mom died. Utah had the appeal of something smaller—calmer."

"You were fourteen by then?"

She narrowed her gaze on him. "How do you know that?"

"I asked around when I first saw you. We were seventeen then, but the area wasn't as big. You were new to me, mostly because I hadn't paid attention until then."

The smile that formed on her lips told a different story now. One of hope and remembrance. "I started at West Gulch High School my junior year. It's no wonder you hadn't seen me before then."

"I remember the first time."

"You're full of shit, Matthews."

Now he moved in closer to her and touched her cheek. "No I'm not. I remember very clearly."

Her lips trembled now. "We hooked up when we were seniors."

"Yep. It took me that long."

"I didn't know you until then."

"I blended into the walls well."

Lacy worried her lip. "You mean to tell me you actually were attracted to me?"

"Yep."

"I had sex with you in the back of your car the first time you even kissed me."

"Lucky me," he said as he stroked her cheek.

"Doesn't say much for a girl who does something like that."

"Doesn't say much for a boy who would expect that."

"We didn't last."

He brushed her lip with his thumb. "That wasn't my fault."

She took a breath as if to argue, then stopped. "I broke up with you."

Declan eased back. "I don't think we ever really broke up. It was as if you forgot I existed."

He watched as her eyes filled with those threatening tears again. "I did do that. I pushed you away."

"You pushed everyone, Lace."

"I'm sorry," she said softly as the first tears fell and Declan brushed them away with his thumb.

"You're here now. I'm here now and I have a lot of feelings for you, Lacy Pratt. A lot."

"We have to finish this case." She winced. "*I* have to finish it. I can't be sitting here talking about what we had fifteen years ago. I need to be out there finding the person who killed your sister."

Declan cupped her face in his hands. "You will. And I'm going to help you do it. But first I want to tell you something."

He watched her eyes go wide with absolute fear. "Don't you dare. Don't say words you can't take back and you very well might not mean."

"You think I'd say them without validation?"

"Just don't." She batted her eyes as if pleading. "Not now."

He pulled back and nodded. "Okay. It's there, Lace." He dropped his hands. "Let's finish this."

Lacy rose from the couch and paced the small living room. She bit on her thumb as she did so. "Vaughn slept with all those women, but he didn't kill them."

"Established."

"Our killer is sending our victims letters."

"That's a mistake on their part."

"He has a point to make," she said looking up at him.

"Right."

She continued to chew on her thumb and walk in circles as she thought. "Autumn Taylor's husband doesn't seem like the kind of guy who gets counseling when faced with his wife's infidelity."

"You make that connection when he punched you?"

Lacy chuckled. "Something like that." She stopped her pacing.

"Sean Cartwright is heavy into the church and we know he's talked to Pastor Ralph about his wife. But what about Tom? Has he sought out counseling?"

"He hasn't said he has. Did my sister seek counseling?"

She cocked her head and stared at him. "I don't know. She never told me. What are you getting at? Do you think that this is linked to the counseling being given by Pastor Ralph?"

"There's a running theme here, Lace. Pastor Ralph's secretary is his wife."

"Convenient."

"She'd know everyone that came to talk to him, but now she's up and left to go to her sister's."

"But never went. Someone else has to know who comes and goes from the church. Someone that could identify Olivia as another woman having an affair with Vaughn."

"That church is always full of people. Cleaning crew. Office staff. Other parishioners. But only one secretary. And that secretary is having an affair with Vaughn."

He saw the heat move up her neck and into her cheeks as she began to put it all together. "You don't really think that Oliva Burton would do all this to cover her own tracks do you?"

"Consider this too. They were both in Seattle when your mom was killed. She had an affair too."

Her eyes went wide, as if she'd never thought about it. She lifted her hand to her hair and tucked it behind her ear, but he noticed it shake.

"That was a long time ago, Matthews. My mother has nothing to do with this investigation."

"And you're trusting the people who were around then too. Do you really think Olivia Burton would disappear and lie to her husband if she didn't have a reason?"

"Such as murder?"

"You said it yourself, the victims knew their killer. Who would run from Olivia Burton?" he concluded.

"People who murder do it for some sick reasons. Maybe she's scared. Maybe she's in hiding. Maybe she has a bigger list of women than we do," Lacy countered, but her voice shook.

"And she might be going after another victim."

She bit down on her thumb again. "Or she is our next victim," she said cautiously, still not completely convinced that the Olivia Burton she knew could have been responsible for her mother's death

Lacy hurried toward her bedroom, changed her clothes, and picked up her keys from the table, all the while Declan stood there watching her sporadic movement.

"Let's find out if Carley Francess-Hastings' husband has any information for us," she said as she headed for the door.

"Like a letter from our killer?"

"Yeah, and then we need to find out what Father Ralph has. I think the time for hurt feelings is over. If we can't find Olivia, then he needs to know what's going on."

"Lead the way, boss."

❧ 26 ❧

They were enroute to find Josh Hastings, Carley Francess-Hastings' husband, when Carl called Lacy.

"What's up, Moss?"

"A missing person's report has just been filed for Olivia Burton. Her sister filed."

"Does that mean she's tried to find her?"

"She's in town. Says after your visit she tried to get in touch with her sister, but no luck. Deciding to take the high road, she drove here and went straight to her house. Burton told her he hadn't seen his wife in days."

"He told me she was with her sister."

"That's his story. Her sister is here talking to Jeb. He's trying to piece a history together on her."

"Looks like I'm headed to Burton's," she said as she took a sharp right and headed toward the church. "I want to get to Josh Hastings and see if he's received a letter from our killer."

"Already on my desk, Pratt."

She pulled to the side of the road and stopped the car. "Didn't want to tell me about it?"

"I've been busy since I came in," he scolded. "I had Stella O'Neal waiting for me and Josh walked in a half hour later."

Guilt squeezed at her. He was getting all the leads while she'd been sitting on her couch sipping wine and eating cheese.

"He got a letter then?"

"Yeah. A detailed account of his wife's affair with Vaughn too."

"So whoever this is had been watching them for a while?" She exchanged looks with Declan who listened to her side of the conversation.

"He went to Vaughn's first. He had every intention of kicking the guy's ass."

"Vaughn is in our care."

"Right, so his ass is safe."

She put the car in drive and headed to the church.

Declan gripped the sides of his seat as Lacy sped through town.

"Don't you need sirens to go this fast?" he asked as she took a corner.

"If they decide to pull me over, I'll have them following me with them on."

"I suppose that's one way to do it. What's our hurry?"

"Olivia Burton has been reported as missing by her sister."

He turned to study her. "I thought her sister hadn't seen her in decades. Why worry now?"

"We seemed to have gotten through to her that Olivia was in trouble."

"But Pastor Ralph didn't report her missing?"

"As far as we know, he thought she was at her sister's house."

He winced as a car pulled out in front of them and Lacy maneuvered around them.

"What about Josh Hastings?"

She took another hard turn and headed toward the church at the end of the road. "Moss has him, and his letter. Our killer is letting us know he's onto us. The fire at Vaughn's, the letters..."

"The fire at Vaughn's?" His voice rose over the squeal of the tires as she came to a stop in the parking lot of the church. "What fire?"

"Someone set a bush on fire and then left him pictures of our victims."

"Shit."

"Yeah."

Lacy swiftly moved from the car as Pastor Ralph pushed open his front screen door and hurried toward her.

"Miss Pratt, what are you doing?" he scolded.

"We have an emergency."

"What kind of emergency?" He looked at her over his glasses and then toward Declan. "Declan, how are you today?"

"Better now," he quipped as Lacy firmed her stance with her hands on her hips.

"Stella O'Neal is in town."

"Yes. We spoke this morning," he confirmed.

"She didn't seem worried to you?"

"Of course she did. She told me that her sister had left her house and she was looking for her. We decided perhaps she'd taken a detour, a scenic route by bus or something."

Lacy pursed her lips. "That's what she said to you?"

Pastor Ralph reached his hand to Lacy's arm. "Darling, what are you getting at?"

She let her stance soften. "Why don't we go inside and sit down a moment."

"I was just headed to my office. Let's head that way," he said as he led them to the door on the side of the church.

Pastor Ralph opened the door to his office and motioned to them both to sit before he took his seat behind his desk.

"Now, Lacy, what are your concerns?"

Lacy steadied her gaze on man across from them. "You said your wife went to visit her sister."

"I did."

"You said she'd picked her up. That's why her car is still here."

"Yes. What's all this about, Lacy?"

She shifted a quick look toward Declan and then back at Pastor Ralph. "I talked to Stella O'Neal yesterday, at her home. She said she hadn't seen her sister in nearly twenty years. According to her, Olivia hadn't been there."

Pastor Ralph's eyes grew wide and he clasped his hands together atop his desk. "But she's not here. She said that's where she was going."

"Stella O'Neal just filed a missing persons report on Olivia."

Pastor Ralph sat back in his chair and placed his hand to his chest.

Declan rose. "I'll get you some water," he said before he hurried out of the room.

"Lacy, my wife..."

"We have reason to think her life is in danger and we need to find her."

"What kind of danger?" his voice shook as he spoke. Declan returned with a paper cup of water and handed it to Pastor Ralph whose hand shook as he took it. "Thank you."

Lacy fisted her hand to keep her calm before she spoke. "Do you know what kind of relationship your wife has with Vaughn Price."

Pastor Ralph took a long sip of water before setting the cup on his desk. He looked down at it, then closed his eyes, and took a long breath. When he lifted his eyes back to her there were tears.

"I can only assume you're asking me that question because you already have an answer to it."

"I mean no disrespect," Lacy confirmed.

Pastor Ralph nodded. "My wife has a bit of a past. Wild child, if you will." He sniffed back the tears, then lifted his glasses and wiped them away. "When we married she was a recovering alcoholic. She had her battles, but in all these years she'd never gone back to the bottle."

"And Vaughn?" Lacy pried.

"I've recently come into the knowledge that she's been seeing Vaughn." He stopped to compose himself. "Seeing him in an extramarital kind of way," he said before taking his glasses off and setting them on his desk.

She watched as the tears now flowed from his eyes and over his aged cheeks.

"I'm sorry," she found herself saying. Watching the man cry was twisting her up inside. "You'll understand that we want to find her. We're afraid that with the current murders, she might be in danger."

He nodded, his lips tightly pressed together as he put his glasses back on. "I've been counseling many families lately. All of them in turmoil over Vaughn Price. I pray for him, Lacy. Why would he do such a thing to these families?"

"He's just a man," she defended.

"But is he killing them?"

"We don't think so. But someone has made him our connection."

She watched as his eyes welled again and his lips quivered. "If I hear from Olivia, I will let you know first thing. Please don't let anything happen to her."

Lacy stood, and Declan followed her lead. "One more thing," she said looking toward Pastor Ralph who slowly rose from his chair, visibly shaken from their conversation. "Have you received any threatening letters?"

"Like the ones Sean Cartwright had?"

"Yes."

He shook his head. "No."

"Sean said you thought it was best for him to tear up the first letter."

"It didn't seem a threat then. You understand. I was trying to help the man."

Lacy nodded. "Thank you for talking to us."

He wiped his eyes again. "Go in peace, dear Lacy. Find the person responsible and bring my wife back to me."

As soon as Lacy backed the car out of the lot, Declan let out a long breath.

"This took a twist, huh?"

Lacy turned the car and headed down the road. "I can't decide if Olivia Burton, her sister, or her husband is lying to us."

"You're thinking that too?"

"I'm siding with the sister," she said as she turned at the light. "The woman told me she hadn't seen her sister in decades. Ralph tells me she picked Olivia up at their home. Then Stella shows up and tells him Olivia left her house? The pieces aren't lining up."

As they passed the parking lot to the walking trails Lacy slowed. "Who is that?" she asked as he nodded toward the man who emerged from the trail and began walking down the street with his hands in the pockets of a black hooded sweat shirt.

Declan shifted in his seat to see the man. "The guy from the coffee shop that used to work with my sister."

"Carter Workman." The name came from her as she turned the car around in the middle of the street.

"What are you doing?"

"He was stalking your sister. Crazy in love with her. But when Autumn Taylor was killed, the only witness said she was in the wooded area with a man in a black hooded sweat shirt."

"Are you shitting me?" he asked as she threw the car in park and jumped out.

"Carter Workman," she called out to the man who stopped mid step and didn't move.

Declan watched as she cautiously walked toward him, her hand on the butt of her gun.

"Can you take your hands out of your sweatshirt? I want to talk to you for a moment."

The young man pulled his hands from the garment and held them up as if he were ready for her to arrest him.

"What have you been up to, Carter?" she asked as she slowly moved to him.

"I took flowers, ma'am. I just did that." His voice wavered, but he didn't move. "I left them on that old fallen tree. That's where they said they found Stacy, and I wanted to leave them there for her."

"Okay, Carter. Will you turn around for me, real slow."

"Yes, ma'am," he said as he did as she asked. "I don't have anything on me except my cell phone, ma'am. I swear."

"Just so we're sure of that, where is your cell phone?"

"In the pocket of my jacket, ma'am."

"I'm going to ask you to remove your jacket, without putting your hands in the pocket. Lay it right at your feet, okay?"

"Yes, ma'am," the young man said with tears in his voice as he did as she asked. "I didn't do anything."

"I understand."

Declan stood at the car and watched as the man did what Lacy asked. He wasn't sure what the hell he was supposed to do if the kid rushed her or pulled a weapon, but the amount of adrenaline rushing though him told him he could take the kid out without a weapon.

Carter pulled the jacket off and did as she had commanded. When it was on the ground he put his hands back up in the air.

"I'm going to ask you to take fifteen steps backward and sit on the ground."

Carter nodded and did as she said.

With her hand still on her weapon, Lacy moved to the jacket and pulled the phone out. "Okay, Carter. You are telling me the truth. Listen, let me tell you why I'm being very leery of you. We have a witness to one of the murders and he was wearing a jacket just like this," she said and even Declan could see the young man's eyes shoot open and the tears stream down his cheeks.

"I've had that jacket for years. I didn't kill anyone," he said. "I swear it. I only came to put flowers on the tree."

"You had a lot of pictures of Stacy Watts on your phone when she died. How come?"

Carter's head dropped and Declan couldn't hear him now. He moved from behind the car until Lacy looked up at him. Her look was searing hot and it stopped him in his tracks.

She moved closer to Carter, still cautious. Declan watched as she reached out and rested her hand on his shoulder as the young man cried. Why wasn't she arresting him? What was she doing?

A few minutes later she stood, as did Carter. She handed him his jacket, spoke too quietly for him to hear, and then Carter Workman walked away.

Lacy watched after him until he was a safe distance away, then she returned to the car.

"You're crazy. He could have killed you or something," Declan scolded as Lacy climbed into the car and he followed suit. "Why didn't you put cuffs on him? Damn it, Lacy, you..."

"You can get right out of this car if you're going to lecture me about my job, Matthews. I had a reason for the suspicion. I acted on it."

"You should have called for backup."

"I did what I did. Innocent kid with a massive crush has his heart broken. Now he has officers watching him. He's not out of my sight, don't think I wasn't backed up."

"At what point did you call for that?"

"Let's just say anything he does we're going to know about."

Declan scrubbed his hands over his face. "I don't know how to handle this."

"Then don't," she said as she shot him a look. "This is how I get things done. If it bothers you then you need to get back to New York."

"Oh, don't do that."

"You're the one with a problem, bud. I saw someone I suspect could have killed three innocent people, I'm going to go after him."

Declan turned his attention out the window. It was more than her hunting down a suspect, and he knew it. How could he be perfectly calm knowing the woman he loved was getting punched in the face or hurt every day when she went to work? It wasn't normal, but then anything with Lacy Pratt wasn't promised to be normal.

✻ 27 ✻

There had been no more words shared between them from the time Lacy stopped Carter Workman until she pulled into the parking lot at the station.

The thought had crossed her mind to take him back to her house so he could get his car. Having him "tag along" today just wasn't convenient anymore.

As she climbed from the car and headed to the door, she turned and threw him the keys. "I'll have Carl take me home when we're done here. You can leave the keys on the kitchen table," she said as she turned back around and hurried toward the building.

But he was quicker, she thought. He'd caught the keys and met her stride. Her temper roared to life when he grabbed her arm and spun her around.

"You're not just dismissing me. Oh, no. You have a handful of leads now, and I'm here for the duration."

"Not a cop, Matthews."

"Lawyer of the accused in your protection," he reminded her. "Vested party in the investigation. Freaked out boyfriend of the detective who takes too many chances."

She sucked in a breath to argue his points, but the word boyfriend seemed to throw her off her game. There was no time for a lovers' spat in front of the station. She had a job to do, and if he wanted to sit on his ass while she brought someone to justice, then he could do just that.

Breaking from his grasp, she continued her walk inside and up the stairs, aware that he was following.

She pulled open the door to the third floor and swiftly moved to her desk. Carl stood from behind his and walked to her.

"What did Burton have to say about his wife?" he asked as he sat on the edge of her desk.

"He said Stella showed up at the house looking for Olivia. He said she said that Olivia had left her house and she was worried about her. He continued to say that they figured she took a bus, or a scenic route. At first he didn't seem to be worried."

"If he wasn't worried why was she here filing a missing persons report?"

"Doesn't add up, right?" she asked as she saw Declan move toward them. "When I told him about our thoughts that she was in danger, he had enough sense to put it together. He knew about his wife's affair with Vaughn."

"Ouch," Carl said, exchanging a glance with an angry faced Declan. "Seems as though Vaughn isn't the only common thread here."

"That's what's throwing us off. Vaughn was with all the women. He's our most common thread. But then there's Sean Cartwright, who has confided in Pastor Ralph about the affair and the letters. Pastor Ralph's own wife had an affair with Vaughn."

"Did he get a letter?"

"No," she said, shifting a steely glance toward Declan who sat silently in the chair in front of her desk. "If Olivia has a hand in this, no reason to out herself. But what if Stella knew about it? What if she did know where Oliva was the whole time and this is some twisted revenge for her sister's poor choices in life."

"You're actually considering Burton and O'Neal as suspects now?"

"Yeah," she said moving past them and walking toward the break room. Carl had put an entire box of Cokes in the fridge, she was helping herself to one, and he wasn't going to stop her with the pettiness of needing them all for himself.

When she turned, Declan was leaned up against the doorjamb.

"You still here?" she snapped.

"Just came to say goodbye. I'm taking your car. It'll be parked at your house."

"Good."

"Before you get all bent out of shape, you should know I'll be texting you a few times tonight to check on you."

"You don't need to do that," she said pulling open the Coke and taking a long, satisfying swig.

"I want to do that." He walked toward her. "You're going to make sure to answer me, too."

"I'll be busy."

"Not that busy." When he reached his hand to her cheek, her first reaction was to flinch and pull back—she refrained. "I'm getting out of your way. I have some work to do myself."

"You'd better check flights too. It's going to get expensive if you don't plan."

Declan ran his tongue over his teeth. "You're bound and determined to make this so hard I walk away, aren't you?"

She shrugged. "Can't believe you're still here."

A smile formed on his lips, and it irked her to the core. "I'm not going anywhere, Pratt." He closed the gap between them. "I'm here for the long haul. Get used to it."

"I'm about to solve this. The haul is almost over."

He snorted out a laugh. "Then you don't get what I'm saying at all." He turned back for the door. "I'll be in touch. Make sure you answer when I text you." And then he was gone.

She stood there, the open Coke in her hand. Certainly he didn't mean the long haul as in her—them. His life wasn't in Utah anymore. Central Park West, she reminded herself. That's where he lived. Gyros and park views. Pizza places on the way home that reminded him of *home*.

Taking another swig from the Coke, she headed back to her desk.

Carl was seated at his desk, the phone receiver to his ear.

She sat down and scrolled through her email.

A moment later Carl moved from his desk and motioned to her to follow. "What's the hurry?" She jogged after him as he headed for the stairs.

"We just got a call from Sean Cartwright. Amy never made it to work today. Her boss called Sean to see where she was."

"We have guys on her. They should have seen her," she said as they hurried down the stairs. "Did you follow up with them?"

"Wish I would have thought about that," he scoffed as they walked out the front door. "They said she parked her car in the lot and went into the building."

"Crap." She pulled open the door to the car and slid inside. "We're still looking for someone they all know. Where's Vaughn?"

"They still have eyes on Vaughn. He hasn't left his house at all. We have two guys outside his house and one inside with him. Literally sitting at his kitchen table with him playing chess."

"We need someone in the wooded area," she said looking at her phone contacts.

"Already called in. I got a lot done while you were having a fight with Declan in the break room."

"I wasn't having a fight," she snapped and he laughed.

"Yeah, you were. You're in love with the guy and you're pushing him away. He's a good guy, Lacy. Give him a chance."

Did all the men in her life need to argue with her right now? She took a breath to combat Carl's ideas as they pulled up to the parking lot where Amy Cartwright's car was parked.

She and Carl both climbed from the car and moved to the officers standing at Amy's car.

"What did you find?" Carl asked.

"Nothing," Dobbs, a rookie traffic officer said. "The car is locked. There's no sign of struggle."

"And her boss reported her missing?" Lacy asked as she skimmed her way around the car.

Carl nodded. "Yeah. Looks like she intended to go in."

"So she didn't make it from her car to her desk. What floor does she work on?"

He looked at his phone for the notes he'd taken on it. "Second floor. She works reception. She would have had to walk right in the door and up a flight of stairs."

"What kind of surveillance?"

"Old building, Lacy. There is no surveillance."

She looked around at the adjoining buildings. But she didn't see anything that looked as though it might be a camera pointed toward the lot.

"Let's head to their house," she ordered, moving back to Carl's car. "I want to know who's been in touch with Sean and Amy Cartwright lately."

❧ 28 ❧

Declan set Lacy's keys on the kitchen table, just as she'd asked him to do. On the drive he'd made a few phone calls, and perhaps the biggest decision of his life—aside from leaving Utah and moving to New York fifteen years ago.

Lacy was in a mode, he thought. This was something he could get used to, though the danger part didn't thrill him in the least. But they'd learn to work together. That's what a true relationship was all about, not that he'd really known what a true relationship was like. His marriage had been a farce from the beginning. They were both to blame for that fiasco. Though, had he known his ex-wife's true bitch potential, he never would have married her.

He'd called Angie and had her arrange a meeting with the partners at the law firm for early next week. He'd fly out for a few days and quit face to face. Then he'd called Patricia, his real estate agent—ex-girlfriend, if he could even call her that. They'd quickly had a conversation about selling his condo, or leasing it out. He liked the thought of some extra income, especially since she had someone already in mind who was looking for just that kind of opportunity. They agreed to meet when he was out in the next few weeks.

When he had more time, he'd arrange movers and look into getting licensed in Utah. He'd made up his mind. Clark Gulch was just the right size for him to start his own firm. In time, he'd convince Lacy that they had a future. One thing was for sure. Her mood swings weren't going to put him off.

He needed to be back home. This was how it was supposed to be, he decided. Fifteen years with a park view was what most people dreamed of. But wasn't it funny, all those years looking over the park, he'd dreamed of home.

As promised he pulled his phone from his pocket and texted Lacy. *Making sure you're okay and Carl is taking care of you.*

His lips twisted with a smile knowing the return text, if he got one at all, would be snippy and probably filled with irritation at the insinuation that Carl would have to take care of her.

When his phone buzzed it was a text from her. *I'm fine.*

Short sweet and to the point, he decided, and full of irritation because he knew her well enough. He laughed as he sat down at her kitchen table with his laptop. The thought of going back to his parents' house hadn't appealed to him. He needed a few moments alone because something had been itching his lawyer senses all day long.

Perhaps it was good that Lacy had sent him away. But since they'd met with Pastor Ralph that morning, Declan had been aching to look into Lacy's past just a bit more—or more specifically, her mother's.

He started his search by looking up information on her mother's death, outside Seattle. Articles about the young boys who had found her came up in the search. Declan made notes of the names in the article, searched those people, and it led him to another article which he found rather interesting. *Third Unsolved Murder in Three Months*, the article was title and that caught his attention.

Patricia Pratt, Lacy's mother, was the third woman to be

found in a wooded area just outside Seattle. All three victims were in their thirties and had all been strangled. From what he'd gathered, all three murder cases were cold as a killer had never been caught.

But what about the man Patricia Pratt had had an affair with, he wondered. That took a bit more digging to find the seventh-grade history teacher who had committed suicide after his wife and kids moved away to Iowa. However, the name didn't come up with any others on his search list, so he wasn't sure how they'd relate.

Declan felt his chest tighten when he read the obituary for Patricia Pratt and realized that Pastor Ralph Burton was the officiant at her funeral.

He ran his hand over his stubbled chin. It wasn't a shock, Lacy had said that Pastor Ralph was part of their life in Seattle, but he now wondered what was Pastor Ralph's life like while in Seattle?

With that, he began to search on the man who held everyone's secrets. He'd been clergy for going on thirty-five years. A career that started in New Mexico, then moved to Saint Louis, and then to Seattle was an honorable one. He was a volunteer firefighter in Missouri. He had a vast knowledge of wilderness survival, which had come into some use in Washington, and that was when Declan's search led him to some interesting information.

Seattle victim number two, Carla Mills, had been found by none other than Pastor Ralph Burton and his new wife Olivia while they were on a hike.

His skin broke into goosebumps and a chill went down his spine as he typed the name Olivia O'Neal-Burton into the search.

There was a jackpot to be had with this one, he thought. What had a man of God wanted to marry a woman on the wrong side of the law for? The list was long. DUI. Drug possession. Petty theft. Identity theft. Had Ralph Burton saved her soul, he wondered?

The list had stopped in Seattle, which had meant that once

they moved to Clark Gulch, Utah, the new Mrs. Burton walked the walk of a pastor's wife—until she fell in with Vaughn Price.

Tapping his fingers to his chin he wondered how much of this Lacy had already looked up. Olivia Burton was with Ralph in Seattle. She was with him when they'd come across the body of Carla Mills. Had she known where to look? Were they just chasing twenty-year-old shadows?

He typed in the name Carla Mills to his search. There were no surprises to find that she seemed to have a list as long as Olivia's. It all seemed a little too tidy now. She'd had a long clean and sober run, but Declan was afraid that the missing Olivia Burton wasn't in any trouble. He was quite sure that maybe she was the one causing the trouble. By the information he'd found he was sure this was a case of jealous lover revenge against the other women Vaughn was seeing. Maybe Olivia Burton was in love with Vaughn, and this was the only way to get him to herself. Although it included his sister, and that had his veins hot with fire. But it didn't tie up loose ends in Seattle. He sat back in his chair and gave it some thought. If Olivia Burton were killing these women because of her relationship with Vaughn, could she have killed Lacy's mother? He sat up and felt the bead of sweat as it formed on his brow. What if she were a jealous wife, and Lacy's mother had been taking up too much of Olivia's husband's time? Maybe it wasn't about Vaughn at all. Maybe it was about Ralph and his connection to these women who had affairs. What if Ralph Burton wasn't made of steel either? That certainly would give Oliva cause to go on such a spree—no matter how sick it was.

Declan closed his laptop and picked up his phone to call Lacy. No, he thought better of it. He'd head down to the station and tell her what he thought, that way he had her attention.

Tucking his laptop into his shoulder bag and headed toward the front door when his phone buzzed with a text message.

As he pulled his phone from his pocket he heard a crashing sound coming from the back yard.

"What the hell?" He walked back through the kitchen, setting the bag on the table.

Walking to the back door, he could see the lights flickering in the garage where Lacy had her workout equipment. Engaging the flashlight on his phone, he opened the back door and started toward the garage.

"Who's out here?" he called out and wished he'd thought to take a weapon of some kind with him. He'd remembered seeing a set of karate sticks, though he couldn't think of what they were called, sitting by the door in the garage. If he could manage to get one in his hand, he'd feel better about walking out to the garage as the lights turned on and off again.

"Come out here," he shouted as the lights turned off.

He looked around the yard. Surely it was an electrical malfunction. Perhaps the crashing he heard was someone hitting an electric pole or something of the sort.

The light came on again and Declan advanced to the door. Peeking inside he saw that the home gym had certainly been tampered with. The heavy bag swung from the rafters. Weights were off the rack and on the floor. So the crash had come from inside the garage, but he didn't see anyone there now.

Probably some stupid kids screwing around, and of all nights, the night his nerves were already shot and the woman with the gun wasn't home. A good thing for them, he supposed, as he turned around to leave the gym and walked right into a set of hands which pushed him back and to the ground. The force was great enough to have him on his ass, and his head bouncing off the concrete.

"What are you doing here?" His voiced cracked as he tried to scramble to his feet.

The lights went out as a foot came down on his chest.

"Lacy will be home any minute. She'll shoot you. It doesn't matter who you are," he warned.

He saw the white toothed smile in the dark as something hit him in the side of the head and his vision went black.

29

Lacy leaned back in her desk chair and rubbed her hands over her face. She hated days like this. Their list of leads had grown, but so had their list of missing persons, and that twisted her gut.

There had been no word on Olivia Burton or Amy Cartwright. They had a heavy presence in the wooded trails and all around town. But there was a part of her that worried at any moment they were going to have another body on their hands, and she didn't want that.

In the past three hours they'd had to send medical to Vaughn's house to sedate him because he was having panic attacks. If nothing else, Lacy figured his days of wooing married women were over.

Carl had accompanied Sean Cartwright to get a cup of coffee and something from the vending machine in the lobby. No one wanted to be home when people were going missing. She didn't blame them.

The thought had crossed her mind to call Declan and have him bring her some clean clothes. It didn't look as if she was going to get home any time soon, and she was wanting a new shirt since at some point it looked as though she spilled either coffee or Coke on her current shirt.

As she picked up her phone, she thought better of it and set it back on her desk. It had already become too easy to just think Declan would be there when she needed him. Hadn't she sent him away while she was busy solving a case that didn't seem to be going anywhere?

And why had she done that? The ache deep inside of her told her she already missed him. How stupid was that? He was still in town. It wasn't as if he'd flown off to New York that night, but she knew he would, sometime, and that started her panic all over again.

God, she wished she had her car. If nothing else, she could drive through Burger King and get some onion rings, which she was craving at that moment.

Her phone buzzed on her desk, and she was sure it was Declan following up on her. The text back was going to be short and snide, she already knew deep in her heart she couldn't give him more than that. It wasn't in her makeup to be sweet and sentimental. He'd been right. She was going to push until he didn't want to come back, even if that wasn't what she wanted at all.

When she looked at the text it was from Declan, just as she'd figured. But when she read it, he wasn't making sure she was okay.

Meet me on the trail at Devil's Fork. I have some information for you.

What in the hell was he up to?

She thought of the trail which started at the parking lot, curved at the tree where they'd found Stacy, and headed toward Devil's Fork before going under the Thompson Bridge.

So Declan hadn't gone home as he said he was going to. And wasn't it Vaughn that had said he ran that way when he'd run those trails. Was this why Vaughn was all worked up? Was he talking to Declan? What had he told him? What did he know?

She pulled her gun from her desk drawer and holstered it on her hip as Carl and Sean walked back toward his desk.

"Give me your keys," she ordered.

"Where are you going?" Carl asked as he pulled his keys from his pocket.

"I have to meet Declan," she said without filling him in. There was no need to pull him into what was going to be a fight she knew. She was mad now. He had no right to get in the middle of her investigation. "I'll bring it right back."

"Be careful."

She gave him a nod and headed out of the station.

LACY DROVE PAST THE PARKING LOT THAT LED TO THE WOODED trails where the bodies of their victims had been found. She noted the police detail there. No one was dumping a body tonight, that was for sure.

She drove another mile up the road and pulled to the side when she saw Declan's car at Thompson Bridge. She'd backtrack to the fork where Declan told her to meet him.

I'm here, she texted. *I'll be to you in five minutes.*

As she climbed from the car Declan texted back. *I'm waiting.*

The path was dark and she now wondered why he couldn't just tell her what he'd learned. Why did he have her on the path? If he had been talking to Vaughn, and Vaughn sent him here, maybe he did know something. Maybe Vaughn was responsible. What if he was setting Declan up?

Her pace quickened toward the fork where the paths converged from three different paths.

"Declan?" she called out to the shadows.

A breeze blew through the drying leaves on the trees, and the fall air chilled her arms.

"Declan, I'm not in the mood for games. Where are you?"

She could hear the sound of someone running, just a steady pace, just as if they were out taking a run.

"Hello?" she called out as a figure of a man ran toward her with reflective stripes down the sides of a dark jacket.

Instinct had her pulling her gun and aiming it at the man who continued toward her.

"Stop. I said stop!"

The man did just as she asked, raising his hands in the air. "Lacy? Lacy, is that you?" The familiar voice in the dark moved their hands and pushed back the hood that covered his head. "Lacy, it's Pastor Ralph. Why are you pointing a gun at me?" he asked with his voice as soft and as calm as always.

"Where's Declan?"

"Sweetheart, I haven't seen Declan," he said as he moved toward her. "I came to clear my head. I'm just out for a run." He raised his hands to hers holding the gun, and lowered them. "Maybe you can put that away. You're making me nervous."

"Declan said to meet him here." She holstered her gun. "Why are you clearing your head in the dark?"

Pastor Ralph tucked his hands into the pockets of his sweatshirt. "Olivia texted me a bit ago and said she'd left. As in she'd left me. Doesn't seem as though she's missing anymore."

"She's still a missing person until we talk to her."

"That's what I told her, too. She has a pattern, Lacy," he said as wisely as he spoke about God and religion. "She'll come around. People never change. Oh, they can change for a moment, but not forever. I'm worried for her, Lacy. Worried that she's in some trouble. Or more like she's causing trouble."

"Causing trouble?"

Now he smiled, and that took her by surprise. "I don't like to think she might be behind all of this, but..."

She watched his eyes in the darkness, and even now they were soft and calm. Belief in his God must have given him such strength, she thought, to smile peacefully even though he thought his wife might be a murderer

"I need to find Declan. His car is on the road and he said he'd meet me here."

"I'll walk with you," Pastor Ralph offered. "There's too much going on for a pretty girl to be out here alone."

"I have a gun."

"Yes, dear, I know." He chuckled. "I'm just glad you didn't use it on me."

Pastor Ralph took her arm in his and they strolled, for lack of a better word she thought, up the path toward the road.

"Where's your car?" he asked.

"Declan took it back to my house. I borrowed Moss'."

He nodded then shifted as he looked at Declan's car. "He has a flat tire. Do you suppose he went for help?"

"He texted me and said he was on the path. Why would he not tell me he had a flat?"

"Did he leave anything inside?" Pastor Ralph asked.

Motorists often left notes if they abandoned their cars. He was right. So she looked in Declan's car.

"I don't..." Her words were cut off when something came around her throat and she was pulled backward against someone else.

She reached for the fabric that yanked against her neck and choked her. Gasping for breath she stepped back into her attacker's body. Her vision was clouding, and tears filled her eyes, but all she had to do was get them on the ground.

As the fabric loosened, she stepped back, wound her leg around the man behind her. They both fell to the ground, and she was free of his grasp. Only then did she feel the sizzling electric pain shoot through her side.

Paralyzed, she tried to gasp for air. The hooded figure stood over her, a stun gun in their hand. And the world slipped away.

❧ 30 ❧

Pounding pain rattled her head, and her eyes, though she willed them open, they wouldn't do so. Lacy swallowed, but it hurt. Everything hurt.

The sound of her own heartbeat pounded in her ears and she could taste blood. But as she took inventory of her body, which was cold and bound to a chair, she realized she was alive.

Continuing to bring awareness to herself, she managed her eyes open, only to find that she was in the dark—bitter dark. A basement perhaps, as the air was cold and damp. There was movement that wasn't her own. She trained her ears to listen. Shallow breathing. Someone else was in the room.

She pulled against the restraints on her hands. They were bound to her sides by a rope, or tie that fed under the chair.

Lacy worked her mouth to moisten it, fighting the ache in her throat. "Who's there?" she managed but only in a whisper. "Who's here?"

Perhaps a sob was what she heard now. Someone tried to speak, but it was obvious they too were restrained, their mouths covered so that no words could escape.

Lacy tried to clear her mind and think of what had happened

to her. She'd gone to meet Declan. Yes, his car had a flat tire and Pastor Ralph was there. Why was he there? His wife had left.

It was coming back to her.

Her throat was raw because she'd been strangled, or they'd attempted to—just like the victims—just like Stacy. Her heart began to race—just like her mother.

Tears welled in her eyes which burned. They'd tried to kill her. She hadn't seen the face of the person who had done it, but... but there had only been one person there.

She tugged at her hands and it only managed to tighten the rope. Her wrists burned and her pulse throbbed against the ropes that bound her. The chair was tall, a barstool perhaps. Her feet dangled and when she wiggled her toes the burning ache from lack of circulation rose up her legs. Surely if she were to get to her feet, she wouldn't be able to stand.

Lacy moved from side to side. It wasn't a strong chair. If she could get enough momentum to topple herself to the ground, perhaps it would break and she could get the rope free.

For a moment she hesitated as she heard the sound of feet above her. The floor creaked, voices muffled, but she couldn't make them out. The sobbing in the corner grew louder.

If she was going to make it out of the basement alive, she had to move soon. She was a stronger person than her mother had been, and if someone had spared her life only to take it later, Lacy wasn't going to allow that to happen.

※

DECLAN WAS SURE HE WAS GOING TO THROW UP AGAIN AS HE turned the steering wheel and the street lights flickered through the windshield. He batted his eyes against them. He had to get to Lacy. He had to tell her.

Somewhere after he'd been knocked to the ground and hit in

the head, he'd lost his phone. He didn't remember anything, but he knew the face.

Once he'd gotten to his knees in the garage, the smell of his own blood had him vomiting. He had no idea how big the gash on the side of his head was, but it was enough to have left a pool of his blood on Lacy's garage floor.

His car was missing, too. Well he wasn't going to die in the garage. He'd taken her keys and managed to navigate the dark streets toward the station where he'd hoped she was still working. He knew who killed his sister, and who had tried to kill him.

Declan slammed on the breaks as someone walked in front of him. Managing to put the car in park, he fell back against the seat as the door was pulled open.

"Declan?" Carl's voice caused him to turn his head. "Dear, God! You're hurt. You need to be at the hospital." He yelled toward someone walking out of the building. "Get me a paramedic. Get me some towels." Carl turned back to him. "What happened to you?"

"Lacy. Get Lacy," he managed through weak breaths.

"Lacy left with my car two hours ago, Declan. She was going home."

He rolled his head back and forth against the seat. "No. She didn't make it." Lifting his eyes to meet Carl's, he took a long breath. "I think they're going to try and kill her."

"Who, Dec? The person that did this to you?"

"Yes," he gasped. "I think they killed her mother."

A man ran to toward the car with towels and Carl pressed one to the side of Declan's head. "Who? Tell me where I need to go."

"To the Burton's house."

⚜

THE VOICES UPSTAIRS GREW FAINTER. THERE WAS NO WAY TO

know who was up there or when they might try to come downstairs.

Lacy realized her senses were working their way back. The basement smelled of sweat, blood, and urine. Whoever she was hearing must have been there for a while, she surmised as she rocked the chair from side to side. As the legs kicked up on one side and then rocked back to the ground, she realized it was going to hurt like hell when she hit the ground, but if it worked, she could be free.

Blood from her wrists trickled down her fingers, and her side from where she now remembered being tasered now burned. She continued to rock the chair from side to side. The legs lifted further off the ground until finally she and the chair were sent crashing to the ground.

It made a horrible sound as the chair hit concrete and snapped. Her head bounced against the ground and she grunted as the pain shot through her. It was very likely that she'd dislocated her shoulder, but she'd be damned if she'd die like this.

The sobbing in the corner grew louder, and Lacy hushed the other person. They heard the sounds above them as feet shuffled across the floor and then a door creaked open and light filtered down into the darkness from the stairwell.

Whoever stood at the top took one step down before there was a knocking upstairs. They stopped for a moment and retreated, closing and locking the door behind them.

Lacy took a deep, stench-filled breath and kicked her legs to get feeling into them.

One of the legs of the chair had broken off in the fall, and Lacy was able to maneuver the rope free from under the chair and bring her hands, though still bound tightly, in front of her. She picked up the leg which had broken off and held it tightly in her hand. Careful to hold on to the bottom, she noted that the top had splintered into a sharp, jagged end.

Her left arm hung to her side and the pain seared through her making her nauseous. She crawled toward the wall, toward where she'd heard the sound of another. When she reached them, they sobbed.

Lacy ran her hands over the body and up their shoulder until she felt their face and the cloth that shoved in their mouth. She pulled it free as she hushed the person to remind them not to make noise.

"I can't see you," she whispered. "Who are you?" They responded, but it was so faint Lacy hadn't heard. "Who?" she repeated.

"Amy," she said again, only loud enough that Lacy could understand.

"Amy Cartwright?"

"Yes," whispered. "Help us. Help us."

"Who? Who else?"

She could hear Amy cry as she ran her bound hand over Amy's arms and found where she too was bound, her hands to her feet.

"Olivia," Amy's voice croaked as her mouth grew moist. "She's here," she whispered. "She hasn't made any noise for a while. I don't know if she's alive."

"I'm going to look for her. Stay quiet," Lacy instructed.

She shuffled around on her knees, following the wall. Her mind raced. Perhaps she had fallen victim to a different maniac. The person who killed Carley, Stacy, and Autumn didn't harm them. They weren't beaten or raped. Why was she in a dark basement with Amy Cartwright and Olivia Burton? Lacy had been attacked physically, and it was obvious that the others had been beaten just by the smells that surrounded her.

Lacy continued to move until she came upon another body. The skin she touched was cold to the touch, but not bound.

She followed the hand up the arm and to the chest. Placing her hand on the still body she felt for the rise and fall.

"She's alive. Only barely," she whispered.

The feeling in her hands was starting to dwindle. In a moment, she wouldn't be able to try to untie herself.

Again, they could hear the shuffling of feet and voices above them. Lacy moved to Amy.

"Does he come down often?"

"Sometimes. I don't know how long I've been here. I went to work. Someone called my name and the next thing I knew was something shocked me and I woke up here."

They had a method, Lacy decided. This was new and not like the other killings. These were meant to be brutal.

"Has he hurt you otherwise?" Lacy asked trying to find any loose end she could find on the rope that tied her.

Amy cried harder now, and Lacy rested a hand on her knee. "Shhh, we'll talk later."

Now she could hear the voices disperse and the footsteps walked one way and a single set walked back through the house. He would come now, she thought gripping the chair leg in her hand again.

Lacy crawled back to where she knew the chair had fallen. Her hair clung to the blood on her face now and the pain from her shoulder made it hard to stay conscious. With her feet, she pushed the chair toward the area where she'd seen the stairs when the door had last opened. If she could just get it where they might stumble, she could then try to counter attack when they least expected it.

31

Lacy pushed herself toward the wall when she heard the door at the top of the stairs unlock. Her heart hammered in her chest as the knob twisted and the door creaked open.

A flashlight broke through the darkness, blinding her from the man, it was obviously a man, who walked down the stairs. She knew the sound of heavy feet and breath.

He'd stopped a moment, pulled the door shut, and locked it again.

"Lacy," his voice called her name as it had many times in her life and it sickened her. "Lacy."

He stopped at the end of the stairs and kicked the broken chair to the side. "I should have known a rope wouldn't keep you in place."

Lacy gritted her teeth against the pain in her shoulder and gripped tighter to the chair leg she wrapped her fingers around.

He walked to Amy and gave her a swift kick to the side. She yelped, obviously too weak to scream. Then she cried.

"I see she only unmuted you," he said shining the light on the rag that had been shoved in Amy's mouth. "Where is she?" he asked and Amy's eyes darted.

Lacy watched as he shoved the rag back into Amy's mouth then smacked her face.

He turned the light back toward the stairs. No doubt now he'd seen her. "Lacy. Lacy. Lacy." He repeated. "Your mother was a whore. Did you know that?" His voice echoed through the basement and it rang in her ears. "Oh, yes. And did you know she was pregnant when she died?" His voice chilled the air around her as she fought to scream and defend the woman that had been taken from her. "As if one sin wasn't enough."

He moved slowly to her now and his face came into view.

There had been a part of her that had heard the voice and still hoped deep inside that she was wrong. But when Pastor Ralph knelt down in front of her she swallowed back the tears that were trying to force themselves to her eyes.

"Why?" Her voice was hollow.

He smiled. He actually smiled at her as he looked down at the piece of wood gripped in her hand. "You ask too many questions, my dear," he said as his lips pursed and he shoved her back against the wall right where she sat. His hand pushed into her shoulder and she let out a scream which had him smacking her across the face just as he had with Amy.

The piece of wood was still gripped in her hand, but the strength to use it escaped her.

"She kept saying your name as she died," he whispered. "As I wrapped my hands around her throat she cried your name."

Those tears that had threatened broke through. Lacy felt their warmth roll down her cheeks. "You killed my mother?"

His face, now shadowed, showed the hard lines she'd never seen before. There was a blackness that hollowed his eyes. "When a woman lies to her husband and lays with another man, she signs her own death warrant. Patricia did just that, Lacy. She not only laid with that other man—a married man, a father—she was carrying his baby. Now that's just a sin that can't be forgiven." He stood, leaving the flashlight on the floor facing her.

Lacy focused on the sound of his movement and closed her eyes against the bright light blinding her.

"She came to me to confess her sins. Oh, Patricia," he made a tsk noise with his tongue. "I had to rid the world of her sins. You understand, don't you, Lacy?"

"Is that why you killed the others?"

He chuckled as he paced the basement. "I hadn't touched a soul since Seattle. I took that pathetic excuse for a wife and we moved here," he spat out the words angrily. "See the Lord doesn't want his children to lie and cheat."

"But murder is okay?"

She heard him move closer to her. "His hands on this Earth, Lacy. I take care of what needs to be taken care of. Those women in Seattle disgraced the Lord. I took my wife to spare her, and she still disappointed." The thunder of his voice rattled inside her. "Vaughn Price took these women and scorned them. The sanctity of marriage was violated."

"And you're playing God?"

"Hands of God!" He moved swiftly to her, kicking the flashlight away as he did so.

"So why am I here? Why me? Wasn't it enough that you killed my mother and ripped apart my family?"

Ralph knelt down in front of her again. "I took away the sin, but now you're a sinner, aren't you? You're sinning with Declan Matthews just as you did all those years ago."

"That's my business."

"He's a married man," he scolded.

"Divorced."

"In the Lord's eyes a marriage is a marriage."

"You're demented," she yelled so that her voice resonated through the room.

He rose in front of her like a demon rising from the ground, illuminated by the light of the misplaced flashlight. "I will kill you, just as I killed your mother," he threatened. "But I will make you suffer, just as I'm making them suffer for their sins. The others were let off easily. A quick death was being kind to them. I've learned that they didn't pay for their sins if I took them from the earth so quickly, so peacefully. You will all learn from your sins."

"You're wrong. We will survive and you will pay," Lacy growled.

Ralph laughed a deep rolling laugh. "You're broken, Lacy. You can't move. Besides, it's a sad thing what happened to Declan today. You have nothing to fight for."

"Declan was fine when he left me," she growled. "He took my car home. He texted me to meet me on that trail where you found me."

Ralph laughed and it rolled from him like he'd heard a good joke at the bar. "I took his car there, angel. I texted you from his phone. You're not a very good detective, are you?" Humor lit in his voice. "You needed to pay for your sins, and now you will."

"What did you do to Declan?"

"Let's just say he had an accident at your house."

"No." The breakdown was coming. She felt it brewing deep inside her. It was what Ralph wanted, and she was trained to not break down, but it was hard.

He was right. She was broken. How was she going to move on him so she could escape? She was not going to die in that basement, and she wasn't going to let anyone else die there either.

Lacy sucked in a breath of courage and fought against the negative. All along she had known that the person they were looking for was someone of trust. She couldn't have imagined she'd have fallen into that trap as well. She had trusted the man who now stood before her slapping her with his words and his hands.

"My father trusted you," she said. Her voice only a raspy

growl, but it gained volume. "Sean Cartwright trusts you. You're damning yourself," she continued. "If you thought you were saving us all from damnation, it didn't work. You're only condemning yourself to hell." The words now spat from her lips as the tears on her cheeks mixed with the blood and the smell churned her stomach. "They'll find you. You'll rot in prison."

Ralph moved to the flashlight, picking it up off the floor and moved at her with a force that she heard before she could see it beyond the blinding light. As he charged at her she held out the jagged end of the chair leg and as he charged her she thrust it toward him, impaling him in the stomach.

The light dropped and he screamed. "Bitch!"

Lacy scrambled to get her legs under her. Her arm hung at her side and her hands had long gone numb. But she managed out of sheer will to move to him. She took the rope that hung between her wrists and brought it to his throat as he howled from the pain of the wood that had gone into him.

Once again, she heard the sound of footsteps above them. Ralph's screams were still loud, filling the area as he fought her with the rope, but she held as tightly as she could even though the pain that ripped through her began to take her consciousness.

Her voice mixed with his as she screamed and the footsteps grew louder.

A moment later the door at the top of the stairs crashed open and light flooded the room again.

Ralph's voice had turned to grunts as he pulled against her and another flashlight shone into her eyes. She didn't let go of the rope. She didn't stop herself from trying to rid the world of the man who had caused her so much pain.

Then a set of hands came to her, and she eased.

"Lacy, stop. Stop." Carl's voice was in her ear. Carl unwrapped the rope from Ralph's neck and he collapsed next to her.

More light filled the room. Lacy winced from the noise of people rushing into the basement, and the light blinded her.

"You're okay, honey. Take some deep breaths," Carl ordered.

She did as he said. "Amy and Olivia they're..."

"We got them." Carl moved in behind her and she eased against him. "Get medical down here now. We've got three women in bad shape and Ralph Burton."

Lacy swallowed hard as Carl began to untie her hands. "Is he dead?"

"I don't know."

"He killed my mother. He killed women in Seattle. Stacy and..."

"We know."

As he freed her first hand, she felt the rush of blood move into her fingers and it ached as badly as her shoulder which hung to her side.

Panic rose in her again and she turned to Carl who worked on freeing her other hand. "Declan. He killed Declan. At my house."

Carl's hands came to her face and held her there. "Declan is alive. He's in bad shape, but he's alive."

She began to shiver at his words. Tears now poured from her eyes and she fell against Carl again. "I love him. Oh, I love him."

"I know. He feels the same way. Let's get you out of here, honey. Let's get you to the hospital."

❧ 32 ❧

Sitting in the ambulance outside the church wasn't where Declan had wanted to be. He'd wanted to be right there with Carl when he took down Ralph Burton. Truth was, he wanted to get in a few punches himself for what he'd done to him, and to Lacy.

There were three more ambulances waiting, and that gave Declan more than one reason to remember to breathe deeply. Burton had killed before, he had to remember that anything was possible at that moment. What if he got to Lacy? What if they were too late.

With his head bandaged, and the promise of a thousand stitches when they got him to the hospital, he sat and waited impatiently.

He'd heard the shouts and the sounds coming from the house as they'd busted in. Now he waited to see what they'd found.

The first stretcher came out with a woman on it. Declan stood and watched as they loaded Olivia Burton, or who he thought might be Olivia Burton under the bruises and blood, into an ambulance before it sped away.

She hadn't been missing after all, he thought.

Another stretcher was wheeled out and Amy Cartwright, nearly as bloodied and bruised as Olivia, looked toward him before he heard her name called out in the dark. A moment later Sean Cartwright appeared at her side and she wept as they loaded her into the ambulance and drove away.

The breaths he was fighting for came harder now. His heart raced in his chest, and his head pounded from the pain as he stood with intent to walk into the house.

"Sir, we should take you now," a paramedic said gently as she rested her hand on his arm. "You need to be tended to."

"Not until they come out." But he hadn't seen another stretcher come out. No one was coming out. A few moments later another truck arrived—the coroner.

As the two men in the truck hurried out and into the house, Declan sat back down, his legs too weak to carry him.

"No. No," he repeated to himself. "God, no."

That breakdown he'd been waiting for since he'd gotten the call in New York that his sister had been killed had arrived. His body shook, his breath escaped, and the tears came.

Then emerging from the front door, he saw Carl. Lacy's arm slung around his shoulders and he all but carried her out of the house.

Her hair hung in bloodied strands, her face was streaked with that same blood. Her arm was protectively held in front of her by Carl, and she limped as she walked—but she walked.

Declan stood and moved to them, his own vision blurred from the pain and the tears.

"You're okay. You're okay," he repeated as he stopped in front of them and lifted his hand to her chin to look at her in the head-lights. "God, what did he do to you?"

"We have to get her to the hospital," Carl said. "You too. You both are a wreck."

He saw the glint of a smile form on her lips. "I love you. Don't ever scare me like that again," she said, her voice gruff and raw.

Declan laughed. "Me? Oh, honey, you look like shit. And with that, I love you, too."

Carl shook his head. "You two are crazy. There's a better time for this. Let's go."

Carl moved Lacy past Declan as he looked toward the house. "Burton?" he asked and Carl looked back at him.

"They'll get him. He's not walking away this time."

৩৯৩

LACY'S HEAD SPUN. SHE WORKED TO OPEN HER EYES, BUT THE sheer force of doing so made her dizzy.

"Lacy. Honey, wake up," the familiar voice called to her as she continued to stir to consciousness. "Here she comes."

When her vision cleared, she saw her father sitting next to her and it took a moment to remember where she was.

"I'm in the hospital."

He smiled and nodded. "Yes, baby. You are."

She tried to move only to find that she didn't have the strength for the effort needed to do so. Her left arm was wrapped tightly to her, and she could remember that she'd dislocated her shoulder.

Her throat hurt and her lips were dry. "Why am I so tired?"

"They gave you something so you'd rest. You went through a lot, baby." He sniffed. "You need to rest."

"You're here."

He smiled again. "Yes. I'm here. Detective Moss called me and asked me to come."

"He killed her. He killed Mom," she sighed painfully.

Jonathon Pratt wiped his damp eyes and nodded. "I know."

"He said she was pregnant. But..."

He nodded again. "She was. I never told you that part. I guess in light of everything, you didn't need to hate her more than you did."

Lacy bit down on her bottom lip. "I didn't hate her. I hated what she did."

"Me too." Her father ran his hand over her hair. "You're so brave. I don't think I've ever been as brave as you."

"I want to help people. I just want peace for people. That's not what happened. Families..."

"Shhh," he said as her voice rose. "You do help people, sweetheart. You have no idea."

The door opened and Lacy watched as Declan stepped in. "Hey, Pratt," he said with a smile.

"Matthews."

He returned the smile and then looked at her father. "It's nice to see you, Mr. Pratt."

"Declan, you look like hell," her father replied which warranted a laugh from her. "Why don't you sit down. I'm going to go see when they think we can take our girl home."

Declan moved in to take the seat her father vacated. He took her hand and interlaced their fingers. "It's over, Lacy. You did what you said you'd do."

"I killed him, Declan. I took his life." There was no pride in it.

"You were surviving, baby. Thank, God."

"What did he do to you?"

"Barbell to the side of the head. I have some cleaning to do in your garage," he joked, then winced when he laughed.

"Who would have thought he could have been so evil."

"No one. That's how he got away with it."

"What about Amy and Olivia?"

Declan took a deep breath. "Amy is fine. She's beat up badly, but okay. Olivia is going to take a lot more healing. She'd been down there most of the week. She's dehydrated. He hadn't fed her and looks as if he had beat her multiple times a day. Her sister is with her, and I think she'll pull through."

He skimmed his thumb over her bruised knuckles and looked

at their hands pressed together. "Listen, as soon as they clear me to travel, I have to go back to New York."

She closed her eyes so that she wouldn't cry. Hadn't she expected that all along?

Thinking about her father's words assuring her that she was brave, she opened her eyes and looked at Declan. "I knew the day would come. Maybe we will keep in touch this time."

He nodded. "We will. You're coming with me," he said.

"I am?"

"Before all of this happened," he pointed to his head. "I had called and arranged a meeting with the partners of the firm to resign. And I'd arranged to sell my condo, though it's been decided that I'll lease it out. People will pay good money for a temporary view of the park."

"What are you going to do?"

"It just so happens that Clark Gulch, Utah could use a new law firm. It also happens that it's time for me to move back home."

"You're staying?" Her voice was soft and filled with the tears that filled her throat.

"I'm moving in with you, too. You don't get to have an opinion on that."

She laughed and reeled it back when it hurt to do so. "I work long and stupid hours."

"Yeah, and you get yourself into a hell of a lot of trouble too, but I'm willing to deal with that."

"Kiss me, Declan."

He rose from his chair and leaned in over her. Gently he pressed his lips to her cracked and bruised ones.

"I love you," he whispered.

"I love you, too," she said as she lifted her hand to his raw cheek. Those eyes held everything she'd ever wanted to see in a lover and a partner. They held promise, and with him she truly believed that anything he did promise her he'd uphold.

"Declan?"

"Yeah?"

She gazed into his eyes and watched the corners of them crease as he smiled down at her at her worst time. Oh, she did love this man.

"Will you marry me?"

His eyes opened wide and he eased back. It wasn't the reaction she'd been going for, but it really shouldn't have surprised her. Why would he want to...

He shifted until he was seated next to her on the bed, their fingers interlaced again. "There is nothing conventional about you is there?"

"No. So if you're going to say no then just..."

"I wouldn't dream of it—saying no." He pressed a kiss to each of her fingers that tangled with his.

"So are you saying yes?"

"Lacy, if you were my wife, I could see my life being complete."

"For heaven's sake, Matthews, give me a direct answer."

"My name is Declan, and yes, I would love to be your husband."

She let out a small laugh. "Declan. I'll try my hardest, but..."

"It's okay. I guess I'll just be able to call you Matthews now too."

"Detective Matthews."

"It has a nice ring to it."

MEET THE AUTHOR

Bestselling Author Bernadette Marie is known for building families readers want to be part of. Her series The Keller Family has graced bestseller charts since its release in 2011, along with her other series and single title books. The married mother of five sons promises Happily Ever After always...and says she can write it, because she lives it.

When not writing, Bernadette Marie is shuffling her sons to their many events—mostly hockey—and enjoying the beautiful views of the Colorado Rocky Mountains from her front step. She is also an accomplished martial artist with a second degree black belt in Tang Soo Do.

A chronic entrepreneur, Bernadette Marie opened her own publishing house in 2011, 5 Prince Publishing, so that she could publish the books she liked to write and help make the dreams of other aspiring authors come true too. Bernadette Marie is also the CEO of Illumination Author Events.

We hope that you liked this release from 5 Prince Publishing, LLC. Please enjoy the following excerpt from another of Bernadette Marie's titles, now available at 5PrinceBooks.com

AMELIA

Book 1 in the Three Mrs. Monroes Trilogy

AMELIA - CHAPTER 1

God she was miserable

Amelia Monroe rolled up the window on her Ford Blazer as she turned down the dirt road which led to the small church. She'd only been to Parson's Gulch, Oklahoma once, and she certainly hadn't been privy to its back roads.

No, her husband Adam didn't want anything to do with the small town—and now she knew why.

She pulled into the lot of the small church and her heart began to race and a pain in her chest forced her to suck in a deep breath. She'd filed for divorce three months ago. Adam Monroe had lied to her for two years. There had been so much more to him and she'd failed to see it.

Now she sat in her truck, the heat suffocating her, as she watched his other wife and their two children climb from the black limousine and walk into the church.

The bastard had been married, with a family, long before he and Amelia had met. That was the end of her marriage. In that moment, she'd even contemplated killing him, but that wasn't how she did things—she was just angry.

Amelia Monroe had been raised to think calmly and use her

words to fight, not her hands—though she could. She was plenty capable of killing the man. She was a trained martial artist. There were hundreds of ways she could have taken him down.

There had been no need to do that though. A land mine in Iraq had ended his life.

She sucked back tears as she thought about it. Damn it, he might have been a bastard, but she'd loved him. His death wasn't what she'd wanted—not really anyway.

She'd just wanted him to suffer for his lies and his deceptions. She didn't want him to be taken from his children—now that she knew he had them.

But here she was at the funeral of her husband and she'd opted to not be singled out. There would be no front pew in the church. She didn't want a flag or a limo. It would be better off if no one knew she was here.

She'd made the trek for peace of mind and, well, he was her husband. The fact that the attorney wanted to meet with her and Adam's other wife after the funeral also had pushed her to attend. After all, there was a lot to sort out.

Well, Amelia wasn't one to run. She'd hold her chin high and she'd face the woman Adam had lied to first. The children were only four and two. She wouldn't do anything to upset them. There wasn't a need for it. Besides, she knew one thing that the other woman didn't. The day was only going to get worse.

In the front pew of the church sat Adam's *first* wife, her children and what Amelia would assume were her parents. On the other side were his parents.

She'd never met them, but she recognized them from pictures. In fact, only until five months ago she was under the impression they were both dead.

She took a deep breath and let it out slowly as she sat down in the back pew of the church.

A man in a gray tailored suit stood at the end of the pew. "Are you Amelia?"

She held her breath. This wasn't what she wanted. She didn't want anyone to know who she was. With a slow nod she acknowledged that she was indeed Amelia.

"Sam Jackson, Adam's attorney."

The man extended his hand and she shook it. The tension in her shoulders began to slide away. At least this man carried as many secrets with him as she did.

"Do you mind if I sit with you? I don't know anyone else."

Amelia moved over and Sam sat down next to her. "You don't know Vivian?" she whispered and nodded toward Adam's other wife.

"No. My business with Adam was mostly done in Oklahoma City. I never met his wife. Wives." He gritted his teeth. "Sorry."

Amelia clasped her hands in her lap. "Not as sorry as I am."

The small church had filled. The mourners were obviously from the community and had probably known Adam since he was a child. Many had gone to the front and hugged his mother and Vivian. The children, one on each side, stayed close to her.

As the pastor spoke to the congregation, Amelia's eyes were glued to the casket draped with an American flag. She hadn't seen Adam in months. The last time they'd spoken, they'd fought. She'd told him she'd wanted a divorce and he argued with her over it. He said it had all been a big mistake, but she knew that was a lie.

Oh, she'd hoped he'd pay for what he did. This, however, wasn't what she'd had in mind.

She lowered her head and wiped her hand across her forehead.

Sam bent his head down. "Are you alright?"

She nodded. "I'm fine. It's just a bit warm in here."

The funeral was almost over when another woman walked through the door. She looked frazzled as if she'd taken that first dirt road and not the second, which Amelia had been warned about.

She'd been crying—a lot. Sam nodded to Amelia to scoot down and then signaled to the woman to sit next to him. She finally did so.

Amelia looked over at the woman who now was sobbing uncontrollably. She'd like to have cried over him like that too. Wasn't the widow of a man supposed to be in the front row of the church? Wasn't the widow of a U.S. solider supposed to know that she'd married an honorable man? Wasn't...

She let out a long breath as the pastor walked toward Adam's other wife and gave *her* a hug.

There was no reason to cause a scene. Sam was Adam's attorney. He was the only reason Amelia had made the trip. Obviously, Adam thought enough to have left her something and that's why she was here.

She wasn't one to point fingers and make others mad, that was why she'd asked for a divorce. She wasn't the kind of woman to show up on Vivian Monroe's doorstep and tell her that her husband of ten years had been married to her for two years. What good would that have done for his children?

Amelia watched as Vivian's daughter clung to her and her other daughter was held by her grandfather. Anger was quickly creeping into the areas that mourning hadn't filled. How could Adam have done this to his *children*?

The pall bearers stood as the pastor began to walk down the aisle. They carried the casket in a procession and his wife, children, and family followed.

As Vivian reached the back of the church she turned her head and gave Amelia a very knowing glance. One that said *you don't belong here*.

Sam touched her arm. "Are you sure you're okay?"

"I wish you wouldn't have asked me to be here."

"I appreciate it," he said as the woman next to him began to sob even harder.

Sam turned to her. "Ma'am, are you going to be okay?"

The woman, with her blonde curls bouncing every time she tried to suck in a breath, shook her head. "Was that his wife? His *other* wife?"

Amelia felt a pain shoot through her chest. She leaned across, in front of Sam as the other mourners left the church, and looked the woman in her bloodshot eyes.

"Are you Penelope?" she asked through gritted teeth and the woman slowly nodded.

Amelia sat back against the pew as the church emptied out and crossed her arms over her chest.

The first Mrs. Monroe had escorted her husband out of the church.

The second Mrs. Monroe was hidden in the back, as if she hadn't existed.

And the third Mrs. Monroe had walked in late.

Other Titles from 5 Prince Publishing
www.5princebooks.com

Chasing Shadows *Bernadette Marie*
The MacBrides: Logan and RJ *J.L. Petersen*
Never Saw It Coming *Bernadette Marie*
Blissful Disaster *Amy L. Gale*
Victory *Bernadette Marie*
Chasing Her Heart *J. L. Petersen*
Alone *M.J. Kane*
Hope in the Rain *Sandy Sinnett*
The Deja Vu House *Doug Simpson*
We Are From Atlantis *Doug Simpson*
Prez *Lissa Jay*
The Train Robbers *James P Hanley*
Walker Revenge *Bernadette Marie*
Lest We Aren't Forgiven *Railyn Stone*
Broken Hearts *M.O. Kenyan*
Goodnight Kisses *Wilhelmina Stolen*
The Three Stones of Bethany *April Marcom*
Wanderlust *Bernadette Marie*
Holiday Past *Jessica Dall*
Christmas Blitz *Amy Gale*
A Christmas for Chloe *Susan Lohrer*
Restored Hearts *Railyn Stone*
Last Christmas *Lisa J. Hobman*

www.ingramcontent.com/pod-product-compliance
Lightning Source LLC
Chambersburg PA
CBHW030400020726
47493CB00003B/899